SEASIDE STORIES

Also by S. R. Martin Jr.

Natural Born Proud, A Revery 2010

On The Move: A Black Family's Western Saga, 2009

S. R. Martin, Jr.
5 - 2 - 13

For Gail

Library of Congress Cataloguing in Publication Data.

Martin, S. R. (Sennie Rudolph), 1935 -
Seaside Stories

An earlier version of "Cowboy's Dance" appeared in *Obsidian II*, published with permission; an earlier version of "A Good Provider," appeared in *Slightly West*, published with permission; an earlier version of "Anything for Me," appeared in *The Seattle Review*, published with permission.

1. Seaside, California   2. Fiction
I. Title

ISBN - 978-0-9844350-2-9

Published by Blue Nile Press
PO Box 188213
Sacramento, CA 95818-8213
Publication date 2011

An Imprint of Path Press

Manufactured in the United States of America

TABLE OF CONTENTS

A Few Words

Like Jean Toomer's *Cane,* Sherwood Anderson's, *Winesburg, Ohio,* and other works that offer insight on communities--people and deeds--in specific places at particular times, these pieces are snapshots of life I witnessed and participated in, growing up in Seaside, on California's Monterey Peninsula, during and after World War II. Some of those who influenced these glimpses were closer to me than others-- family members and school mates, for example--but all made imprints on me, the place, and the time. No character here is a person I met or interacted with, no happening a record of an actual event. All are "seemings," folks and incidents as they might have been.

I hope you, the readers, the only ones who can validate these efforts, will overlook my failings. I hope you will see, embrace, and share, whatever insights and understandings, what ever consonance with your own experiences, these pieces might contain. I hope in the end these stories will contribute to all of us being reborn, over and over again.

These pictures sample Seaside. There is more, oh, so much more. Perhaps in the future....

S. R. Martin, Jr.

Cowboy's Dance

By the time I got there, most of the fire was already out. Sitting two or three lots off Fremont on one of those little side streets--Park or Palm, or some other name I've forgotten after three years of absence-- the house seemed to crowd the sidewalk and lean towards the street. Huge floodlights washed everything in garish, surreal light, and smoke and steam poured out of the windows and doors. Firemen, looking like space men and carrying axes and shovels, sprayed water and rushed back and forth into and out of the house. The noise from the machinery and hoses was deafening, and the smoke and water made everything smell dank and musty. What was left of his body, looking small, forlorn, laid under a sheet on a gurney at the back of the aid van. I just didn't have the stomach to go see his remains. I had last seen him at the barbershop earlier that day, and now he was dead. Crazy!

Beckwith, the barber, nudged my elbow,

"I hated to get you up, man, but you the only one I could think to call. Cop told me Abe Collins poured gasoline on Cowboy and set it on fire. Said Cowboy's coughin wouldn't let him get no sleep. Abe in jail now." I gave his shoulder a squeeze and thanked him before turning away from the house.

I leaned against a parked car, out of the way, but still with a good view of everything, and thought about the day just passed, and about Cowboy. His death seemed stupid and pointless, like his life. Mom thought he was "simple and generous." The old man said he was "trifling and weak." Now generous and weak were just words. The essential fact was his death.

1

Willie Russell James wasn't really a cowboy. People called him Cowboy because of his incredibly bowed legs. He was five-four, skinny and coal black. His head sat right on top of his narrow shoulders, and his short upper body made his bow legs that much more noticeable. Walking down the street drunk, he looked like a cartoon character, a wino marionette who had leaped off the page into life.

I can't count the times I've passed him standing around talking with other drinkers on the corner in front of Mitchell's Market when other people were working. Drunk or sober, Cowboy would do a little squat every time he spoke. Coming out of the squat, he'd say, "Hot-dog it…" and then go on with what he had to say. I'll never know where that funny little black dude ever came up with a lame curse like "hot-dog it." Maybe he didn't really want to swear at all, but he said it all the time. And when he got to talking fast, he looked like he was dancing: squat—"Hot-dog it," squat—"Hot-dog it."

He was too old to be one of my close friends, but I remember that he'd sometimes interrupt one of our football games by calling for us to throw him a pass, and once or twice on rainy days, he drove Bub and me around on our paper route in whatever old pickup he had back when we were twelve or thirteen. He just sort of hung around my dad's church members; he might even have been somebody's cousin or something. I don't know. From what I could tell, though, he mainly drank. I never knew why he drank so much, but I'd see him stumbling bow-leggedly along Fremont Street or to and from that little house he had shared for years with his wine buddy Abe Collins.

The day of the fire, I went to Beckwith's shop to get a haircut. I was on the Peninsula for the weekend with my folks. I had a deep chest cold, and although I was doing fine at the San Francisco Conservatory of Music and was scheduled to graduate in a few months, I wasn't getting anywhere with my major composition project. I felt depressed,

2

hoping rest and my mom's cooking would help me get pumped up enough to write something better than I had so far. Too restless to keep still though, I finally jumped into my car and ran over to Beckwith's.

As I walked in, the rotund, ginger-colored barber boomed,

"Hey, Music Man. What's happenin'?"

"You what's happenin," I answered, glancing around to see who was ahead of me.

My dad's best friend and hunting partner, Deacon Carl, was in the barber's chair; Ronnie Lewis, a dude I knew all through school sat in one of the half dozen tubular dinette chairs lining two walls of the shop; and a couple eight or nine year-old boys I didn't know, took up two others. Last, there was Mattie Phelps, one of Seaside's most "out" lesbians. I sat down in one of the remaining chairs.

Deke grinned and spoke, Mattie nodded to me and Lewis came over and shook my hand,

"Ain't seen you in these parts for a long time, man. You okay?

"Yeah. I'm in my fourth year of music school up in the City."

"That's cool," Lewis said, raising his clenched fist in a half-salute as he sat back down.

Beckwith's shop looked like a thousand others in Black America—the yard-high posters of well-groomed, light-skinned Black men and women advertising hair straighteners and pomades, the coke machine and checker board, the cheery funeral home calendar wishing customers a happy new year, the old issues of *Ebony* and *Jet*, the small cyclops of a TV set blaring the ubiquitous ball game—this time Shaquille O'Neal and the L.A. Lakers versus the Phoenix Suns—out into the room. The scents of after shave, hair grease and machine oil hung in the air.

Suddenly, the barber muttered,

"Aw, shoot!" I glanced up just in time to see Cowboy ambling

3

unevenly down the driveway.

The door burst open and he lurched in. Once inside the barber shop, Cowboy did his squat, sagged back against the pop machine and mumbled,

"Hot-dog it, they took my ride."
Then he brightened and spoke loudly to everyone except the woman and the kids.

"Hey, Beckwith. Deke. Little Ronnie, Little Ronnie. Carter, my main man. What's happenin?"

The men acknowledged his greeting. Mattie Phelps stared hard at her magazine. The boys drew closer together and kept their eyes riveted on the single one glaring back at them.

Cowboy broke into a fit of coughing that took his breath away. He wiped his eyes with his palms and his nose with the back of his hand.

"I done had this damn cough over a month now. It's kickin my ass, Jim,"
he announced to no one in particular.

"Took my ride," he finished.

He was wearing a light blue jumpsuit much too big for him. He had cinched it tight in the middle with a wide black belt. His thick, uncombed hair was matted all over his head except for two empty spots, and his shoes were tied onto his sockless feet with mismatched laces. There was a damp ring in the crotch of his jumpsuit, and he reeked of urine and wine.

He grinned widely, exposing bare gums where his two front teeth should have been, and said,

"Carter, man, you ain't been in Seaside for a long time. How come you don't come roun' no mo'? I seen your ride parked out in front and decided to come see you for a minute. How you doin?" Coughing and blowing into my handkerchief, I told him,

4

"Feel lousy. Got this awful cold."

"I know what you mean, hot-dog it," he said.

"Better grab a seat," I said, indicating the empty chair between Mattie and me.

"Yeah," answered Cowboy without moving.

He seemed to be trying to figure out how to relate to the barber and his customers. He sort of perked up and started in on the deacon,

"Hey, Deke," he yelled over the din created by the TV's metallic rasp and Beckwith's electric clipper, "you still missin all them deers up yonder in Modoc?"

"Naw," said Deke from the barber's chair. "I didn't see nar one this year. But I'll git im next time."

All the men laughed because everyone knew the deacon hunted every season with my old man, but he was such a bad shot he had never killed a deer.

Still laughing, Cowboy stumbled over to sit down beside me. Mattie Phelps involuntarily pulled her mannish coat more tightly about herself and flinched away from him. Feeling her revulsion, Cowboy turned on her,

"Wha's wrong wit you, Dyke? Scared I'm gon kiss you or sum'pn?' He cackled loudly at his own cleverness.

"What you doin here anyway? This a man's barbershop." Lewis ducked his head and choked off a laugh.

I'd seen Cowboy go off on people when he was drinking, and I didn't want to encourage that, so I looked away.

"Min' yo mouf, Cowboy," growled Beckwith from behind his bushy moustache. Mattie snatched up her purse and jumped to her feet.

"Be back later, Beckwith," she said, moving towards the door.

"Yeah, Mattie," he said, seeming relieved that one less stimulus to Cowboy would be left in the shop.

5

"Derelict," she spat over her shoulder at Cowboy.

"Well, 'scuse me," called out Cowboy, jerking towards me and having to grab hold of my shoulder to keep from falling into my lap. Still leaning over awkwardly, he hollered after Mattie,

"Go 'head, bitch. It's gon take a whole lot more 'n a haircut to make a man outa you, don't care how much pussy you eat."

He broke into his loud laugh, ending in another coughing fit, this one punctuated by the door's slam. I started coughing too.

Deke climbed down out of the chair and fumbled for his wallet. Ronnie Lewis passed behind him into the seat. Deke huskied up his tenor voice and said,

"Cowboy, whyn't you go on 'bout yo bizness and leave these people alone?" Without waiting for an answer, he said,

"See you in Sunday School," to me as he walked out the door.

"Yeah," Cowboy said to the closed door. "I'm on the way down to meet Abe when he finish cleanin up the 101 Club so we can go home and cook sumpn' t' eat. I'm jes talkin to my man Carter for a minute. Yeah."

For a few minutes, the only sounds in the room were the television set barking out the game and Beckwith's electric clipper going over Lewis' head. Suddenly, as if snapping awake, Cowboy turned to me,

"Gotta smoke?"

He caught me off guard and I started coughing again. I finally answered, "Don't smoke."

"Gotta smoke?" Cowboy shouted at the barber, who simply nodded his head in the direction of the long shelf on the wall back of the cutting chairs. The drunken little man maneuvered himself unsteadily to it. Exhaling a cloud of smoke out of which he came coughing, Cowboy said as he passed the chair,

6

"Should git me a haircut too, but my head's too sore." He patted one of the hairless spots gingerly.

"Cop hit me with his stick an put me in jail. An they took my ride. Now I gotta walk everywhere."

"Shoot! If you had of hit my car like you did them three down there on Fremont, I would've hit you up side the head and throwed yo butt in jail too," cracked the barber.

Lewis laughed, but since this was all new information to me, I just smiled and waited to see what would happen next.

Cowboy turned to Lewis in the barber's chair,

"Hey, Ronnie. You still lettin white folks run you roun like them Eyetalian boys useta do when you useta be comin home from school?" Lewis look embarrassed. Cowboy laughed. I was glad to be living in San Francisco instead of this small town where everyone knew everything about everyone else.

Once he'd managed to regain his seat, the little man crossed his bow legs and leaned towards me. Winking up at me and mocking a stage whisper, he said,

"See that little motherfuckuh sittin up there in that chair so cool? Nobody wouldn't never tell you, man, but that little joker never did like you. Your brother neither. Back when y'all was in school an he was playin like he was yo fren? He didn't like you. Said y'all was stuck up an didn't like nobody. Jealous what he was. Why? Cause R'em Hankerson an y'all had them fine clothes an cars an things an went on them fishin an huntin trips an everything."

It was my turn to be embarrassed, so I looked at Cowboy, not Ronnie Lewis.

"I knew he was a lie, an everybody else did too. Y'all likeded me, tho. An yo mama, Mizz Sarah, always useta say to me, 'Come by an see us, Cowboy, you welcome here any time.'" He reared clumsily back in his

7

chair cackling, only to have his laugh cut off by another fit of coughing. When he caught his breath, he hollered out,

"Whoooeee, Little Ronnie, Little Ronnie, yo shit done hit the street."

"Be cool, Cowboy," threatened Beckwith. Lewis squirmed around in this seat.   Whatever he was trying to do, Cowboy clearly intended not to stop until he was completely finished.   In fact, he picked up momentum and swung around to face me, his wine breath making me almost nauseous. It was my turn.

"So you up in Frisco at that big, white music school an you jes come down here to Seaside in yo pointy-toed Floshines every once in a while."

I started to answer him, but my coughing interrupted me. Cowboy went on,

"They like you up there? Bet they don't even think you cullud. Bet they don't even know how everybody useta call you that name yo daddy give you—Satch. Mr. Satch. Mr. Satch Hankerson. Gon be a composer an all. Right on!"

I tried to cool him out, "Hey, Home Boy, it's just me, Carter, the same dude I've been all along. Gimme a break!"

"What you mean, a break? Don't nobody give a nigger no break," he exploded, emphasizing the profundity and finality of his judgment with a sharp head nod.

"But you awright with me, man. Yeah. Leas' we cough jes' alike."
He cackled loudly again.

He paused, his thoughts floating randomly through his wine-soaked brain. My old man called people like that "loose-minded"—not stupid or slow necessarily, but ones whose minds wandered or whose ideas didn't always follow one another closely. Cowboy continued,

8

"'Member when you useta direc R'em Hankerson's choir? Man, y'all was too much. Ole Billy Jenkins be pumpin on that organ—brrummmm-boo-doo-brrummmm—an Cora Davis be addin in that piano—plinkety-plink-plink—jes like a man an a woman doin it: he do "bloo," and she do "wheee;" he do "bloo" and she do "wheee," back and forth like that. An then you, Mr. Carter, Mr. Satch, commence to cut in,

"*Oooo, lawd, lawd, lawd,*" spreading his arms in a broad gesture.
He laughed again,

"Whooooeeee! Ya'll be workin out, Man, and all them fat sistas be jumpin an sweatin an stinkin." I useta come to church on Sunday night jes to hear y'all sing. An sometimes I wouldn't even be drunk neither. Hot-dog it, y'all was bad!"

"Sho was," chimed in Beckwith.
Cowboy kept on,

"Boy we had some good times back in them days. We was good frens. Course I guess now you more closer wit them artises an all up there in that big college and everything."

I didn't object to his recalling our friendship as being closer than I did.

With a slightly backward tilt of his head Cowboy sort of squinted at me,

"How old you is now, twenty?"
"Turned twenty-two back in the fall."
"Hot-dog it," Cowboy mused.

"That mus be right, cause I'm almos thirty, an I'm eight years older 'n you. Be thirty in April."

I smiled at him, though I was getting tired of his ramblings. I even pulled away from him a little.

Cowboy's head rolled forward onto his chest. Exerting substantial

9

effort, he raised it.

"Now here you are, Mr. Satch…Mr. Carter, so talented and all, goin to that big school takin up bein a composer, an here I am still stumblin aroun' Seaside drunk. Somethin happened to me. I don't know what. Jes los I guess. But, man, don't nobody give a nigger no break. Know what I mean? Shit. Jes cause I had a little wreck, white cop hit me up side the head an took my ride. I'm tellin ya, Jim, everywhere you look, the man be steady down on a nigger. Won't give a nigger no break. I mean, no break. But you all right with me Carter, man. Go 'head and keep on workin out. I mean, don't nothin beat a failure but a try. Know what I mean?"

I was silent again, hoping my cool response would finally persuade Cowboy to be quiet.

Henry Beckwith had finished Ronnie Lewis's haircut, so he shook the clippings off the big apron onto the floor while Lewis got out his money. He paid the barber and scurried out the door, saying,

"Later, y'all."

I needed this encounter with Cowboy to be over. In a flash, I jumped up, crowding in ahead of the two little boys who were still waiting and taking turns going to the bathroom. Beckwith hesitated momentarily, but nodded gravely to let me know he understood what was going on as he prepared to drape the apron over me. Passing Cowboy, I grabbed him by the hand, helping him to his feet.

"I got to get me a little trim here, Home, so I can't talk anymore. It was good to see you, Cowboy."

"Yeah. I got to ease on down here to the 101 Club to meet Abe. Hope he ain't too drunk to cook. They took my ride so I got to walk. Drop by the house an have a little drink wit us when you git through here."

"I need to get this cold home to bed, but I might swing by just for

10

a minute,"
I lied, getting into the chair.

He stumbled out the door without saying anything more. On his way past the window on the side of the building, he rapped on the glass with his knuckle, and when I looked up, he gave me thumbs up.

"I don't know how come that boy to mess up his life so bad," mumbled Beckwith, turning on his electric clipper.

"Ain't even thirty yet. All he need is for somebody to dig a hole an cover him up once he fall in it." I didn't answer the barber, but I'm sure he could sense my relief as I settled back into the big cutting chair.

That was the last time I saw Cowboy alive.

The floodlights' blinking twice before going out startled me back to the present. I looked at my watch and saw it was 1:15 in the morning. One of the big fire engines roared away towards Fremont Street, followed by the aid-car-turned-hearse containing Cowboy's body. Cowboy might truly have been simple and generous, or loose-minded and weak, like my old man said, but now he was dead. Stupidly and capriciously dead. It might have been anyone. Me. Crazy. I murmured to myself, "Hot-dog it," and moved off towards my car to head home and read for awhile.

The Silver Kings

It was a quarter to five. Hucklebuck and I were dawdling around in the church-basement cafeteria waiting for Deke to come back from delivering dinners so he could help us clean up. The place was a mess. The gas range and hood dripped grease, the garbage cans spit out potato peels, onion skins and mustard stems, and the Monterey Peninsula sand, kicked around by hundreds of heavyweight steps, scratched the linoleum and drifted under the tables. The comfortable smells and the afterthought of heat from the cooking lingered in the rooms.

A big bunch of the sisters worked hard that Saturday--cooking and baking and wrapping and boxing. They sold a hundred and fifty chicken dinners. Each one included half of a southern-fried chicken, a gob of Irish potatoes creamed with butter and milk, a pile of ham-hock-boiled collard greens, a cup of tossed salad, two biscuits, and a large helping of peach cobbler baked that day. Selling at $1.75 each, the dinners brought in a nice little piece of change to help build the new church.

Lots of people came into the cafeteria to pick up their dinners, but the three of us - Hucklebuck, Deke and I - delivered the rest, and now we were waiting for Deke to get back so we could haul out the garbage, scrub the pots, wash the stove down and do the floors. The primary school children's Sunday School classes met in the cafeteria, and Pastor liked to have it clean for them.

Hucklebuck's name was Henry Strange, but since he'd been known as the best hucklebuck dancer in town before he got saved five years earlier, we still called him that nickname. He was a long, lanky drink-of-water, six-feet-five or something, with copper colored skin, a big, pointed nose and small, slanted eyes. He greased and combed his hair away from a long part beginning over his left eye and running to the back of his head. He bent slightly forward from the waist when he walked, like some tall people do, so he seemed to be bowing with each long, slow stride. And his reticent, gentle manner made him feel easy and approachable.

"Think I hear im comin," Hucklebuck said, unfolding out of the chair he'd been sitting in.

Sure enough, I, too, could hear Deke humming his way down the outside stairs into the basement. He burst through the door with a Monterey Herald rolled up under his arm and stood still, looking around for a moment.

"How come y'all ain't through?" he teased. "Man, long as I been gone, I thought y'all would be done finished the work by now," he said, grinning.

He smiled often and talked with a laugh in his voice. Deke's name was Augustus Carl. He was heavy-set and shiny black, with slicked back hair the color of his skin and sparkling white teeth. He built things and kept an extra, full toolbox in his car trunk. He moved energetically and quickly for such a big man, and he gave off an air of competence and confidence. People could see easily that he was a man who got things done.

He tossed the paper onto a table and steered his bulk through the door into the kitchen, saying,

"Y'all do the pots an' I'll do the stove. Then we can all take out the ga'bage, an mop the flo's."

"Where'd you go?" asked Hucklebuck, moving towards the sink.

"Man, I done been all over. Monterey, New Monterey and Pacific

13

Grove. I musta delivered fifteen or twenty dinners. Made me hongry, so I wanta git on home soon as I can. I'm gon take me home some o' Willie Harrises barbecue an greens. Sugar Ray gon fight on tv tonight an I wanna see im."

"Me too. See any o' the members or anybody?" continued Hucklebuck.

"Naw," Deke answered, "but I seen Pastor's boys on them new bikes he got em. Hee, hee, hee. Man, they was haulin,'high-tailin it. Satch had his head down over the handlebars jes' a'goin, an' Bub, he was pedalin so fas' you couldn't even see his feet. Hee, hee,. Act like somethin was chasin em"

"Where you reckon they been?"

"I don't know, but I thought I heard Sista Sarah tell somebody they was gon ride they bikes up to the high school in Monterey to go swimmin. All I know fer sho is that Pastor's over to Fresno fer that preacher's meetin."

"Man them boys an them bikes is somethin," Hucklebuck said, filling the deep sink with soapy water to use on the pots.

"You dry, Brotha," he said to me. We started to work.

Huck was right about those boys and those bicycles. The bikes sure were pretty. Prettiest ones I ever saw. Made out of stainless steel or chrome from front to back--fenders, tubing, wheels, everything. And fat, red-walled, balloon tires and white, wooly seat covers. Pastor Hankerson called them Silver Kings, and said they were the only ones on the Peninsula. He saw a picture of one in a magazine somewhere and decided his boys had to have them. They were expensive, too, over $200 apiece, but he got those boys whatever he could afford, and some things he couldn't. Crazy about his boys.

And those boys loved those bikes. I think Satch must've been about thirteen so that would've made Bub about eleven. You'd see them

14

all over, riding and grinning. Sometimes, they'd let other kids ride them a little, even that skinny little white boy that lived next door to the church, but mainly they kept those bikes to themselves. Everyone knew those Silver Kings were something special.

Deke came out of the kitchen into the dining room to put his hat on the table with his paper. He hesitated, then hollered,

"Hey, y'all, come ere! Look at this!" Over a half-page picture, the headline blared "BOY KILLED BY SHARK OFF LOVER'S POINT."

"Oh, my Lawd," Hucklebuck murmured. "Ain't that somethin?" We gathered around Deke to get a good look at the paper.

The picture showed a pale, white male form, wearing only swimming trunks. It was lying on a blanket. Two dark, jagged gashes tore into the right thigh in a line ripped through the boy's flesh. According to the news account, the boy was swimming in the ocean when the shark, apparently attracted by his color or his splashing, took him for food or an enemy and attacked. The fish's teeth severed the boy's femoral artery, and the kid bled to death almost instantly. People stood around the dead boy, wonderment and sadness in their faces.

"Ain't that somethin'?" Hucklebuck murmured again. "Musta happened while you was over there, Deke." We all looked at the picture and read snatches of the article.

"Oh, me," Deke blurted out. "Look, y'all. The boys! Thas why they was in such a rush when I seen 'em. They was scramblin to git back home to Seaside."

He was right. There in the crowd of shocked onlookers were Satch and Bub Hankerson. In among the policemen and doctors and ambulance drivers and everybody. Satch's eyes in the picture were bucked wide and his mouth hung open as he stared down at the body. He was straddling his Silver King, gripping the handle bars, looking like he had got there in a hurry. Bub looked worried and had a hold of Satch's arm as if trying to pull him away. A pall hung over the crowd in the picture and over the men in the church basement.

"What you reckon them boys was doin' way over yonder in Pacific Grove?" Huck asked.

"Aw, man, they was swimmin." Deke answered. "They didn't go to no high school. They went to P.G. to swim in the ocean. They liable to been swimmin' wit' that dead boy."

"Ya reckon?" from Hucklebuck.

"Sho, man," Deke put in. "They jes tol they mama they was goin to the school. But they in a world o' trouble now. Rev. gon blister they ass when he git home."

"You ain't s'pozed to say ass no mo, Deke. You saved now." Hucklebuck corrected him.

"Hee, hee, hee," Deke laughed. "Whatever it is, Rev. gon heat it up when he git back to town. You can b'lieve that. "We all laughed, but the sadness on both accounts settled in among us.

Huck looked down at the picture of the dead kid, the crowd and the Hankerson boys, shaking his head slowly.

"I hope not. Maybe he won't find out," he said hopefully, almost as if to himself.

"What you mean?" Deke came back. "You know he always read the paper first thing when he git home, don't care how early or late it is. Been doin it ever since I been knowin im. Thas how he know all about them Roossians, an Africans, an all them folks everywhere else he know so much about. Rev. read a lot, an he start wit the paper."

"But I don't spect Sista Sarah gon let 'im whup em," Hucklebuck persisted. "Might jes punish em some other way. Seem to me they done already been punished, seein that dead boy, killed right close to em an all."

"I remember once back home in Alabama, my daddy sent me an

16

my brother Willie, the one jes under me, to the plantation sto in town to get some flour and some seed fer peas. I was 'bout leven an Willie was bout nine. We heard they was a mob that done something to a cullud boy name Jessie. He was bout my age. We knew him, but we didn' know whether the story was true or not.

"So we drove the mule pullin the wagon the seven miles into town. Got there, and sho nuff they was a big crowd o' folks standin around lookin up in a big ellum tree. There was Jessie, hangin there, all shot up. His neck was broke an his dick and balls was hangin out his mouth.

"Man, I turned that wagon around and headed straight back home as fast as I could. Didn' git nothin Daddy sent us for. Made me so sick to my stomach I had to jump down off that wagon an vomit. I vomited so much I stopped bringin up anything but nasty, bitter green stuff. Willie, he cried all the way back to the place, and when we got there, he run in the house an squatted down in a corner an didn't do nothin or say nothin but cry for the rest o' the day until way over into the night. Mama finely got him to take some cornbread an milk that seemed to settle him down some. Mama and Daddy didn whup us or nothin cause we'd done seen enough."

"Look like that white boy the shark killed was bout Satch and Bub's same age. They seen enough to stan fer punishment."Deke argued back,

"Age don't matter none. Folks dies at all ages, you know that. Don't you remember them three little chil'rens burned up in that fire out to Marina las' year? When yo time's up, yo time's up. Naw, man, them boys wanted to ride them bikes far as they could, so they jes told they mama a story, like all kids do sometimes. An Rev. don't hold wit no lyin, not in nobody. Them boys gon git it."

"Prob'ly so, but don't seem right somehow. I mean, Rev the one

17

went out an bought them fancy bikes. Had to have em for his boys. Proud an everything. Act almos like white folks. Yuh know?"

"Shoot. You know Pastor. He do whatever he wanta do, long as he think it's right. If he wanta do somethin an got the money to do it, an it don't hurt nobody an ain't a sin or nothin, he jes do it. Long as he think he doin right, he don't care what nobody think. He don't care one way nor another bout white folks. Nobody else neither. Thas jes how he is, man, independent like."

"I guess so, but I jes hate to see em git a whuppin after what they been through, seein that dead boy an all," Huck mused.

"Me, too. An it's a shame about that boy. But they got to learn that tellin the truth count, cause ya never can tell what's gon happen one minute to the nex. Like the ol folks say, 'can't learn no younger.' When they done growed up, they'll remember that chicken-dinner Saturday when they tol they mama they was goin to the school to swim but didn't an rode them silver bicycles to Pacific Grove an seen that white boy killed by that shark."

Then Deke laughed, "An the whuppin they got."

Deke turned his big body away from the table, back towards the kitchen, and said, "C'mon, Huck. I'm hongry. Les git through so we can git on home. I wanta eat an see that fight."

Hucklebuck lingered over the paper for another long moment, then pulled back slowly, saying, "I guess you right."

"Sho, man," Deke called over his shoulder. Then we got busy.

18

Privacy

Next to sex and money, the Hankersons struggled with each other most about their boys. Since he was a holiness preacher, Booker was quite severe regarding the boys' leisure time, not letting them go to ball games, movies or dances, and he refused to buy a television set. He called it "bringin the picture show into the house." He even insisted that the boys listen only to church music on the radio. His wife, Sarah, thought he was too rigid, and with flashing eyes would declare,

"They have to be able to do some of the things other kids do. You're the preacher, not them."

He wouldn't argue back. He'd just get that look in his eyes like he was staring intently at some object way off in space. At those times, she might as well be talking to a stump.

Besides, his temper was even worse than his wife's. While she might fly off the handle in a flash, just as quickly, she was over her explosion and on to the next thing. Booker's rage, though, would smolder for days and weeks at a time. When he did blow, he did so in a big and ugly way.

Once when Sarah let Satch and Bub sneak off to a picture show, Booker had stormed into the Del Rey right in the middle of a cowboy movie , yanked them out of the theater and dragged them home for a whipping. He didn't give a hoot for Roy Rogers or Hopalong Cassidy. And he only growled in response to his wife for two weeks. Sarah never doubted her husband's love for their children; she had simply learned to monitor his disciplining them.

But now Satch had her all out of sorts again. Maybe it really was because he was her firstborn that he was able to irritate her so easily. And his stubbornness was more like his father's every day. Sarah felt a nagging fear that he was drifting away from her. Now he wanted privacy! At fifteen, what did he have to be private about?

He was mad too. It was Saturday and he wanted to be out with his friends playing baseball. She also knew that ball playing was only half of the story. The rest was hanging around up there at Noche Buena schoolyard with all those little gals. Especially that Lena Welles, who already had breasts like grapefruits bulging out her blouses, and who switched her behind around like she sat on the world's most valuable treasure. Sarah and Booker decided Lena was too old for her age, "too much company," as they put it, and resolved to keep Satch from getting too close to her.

Sarah staggered to her and Booker's bedroom and collapsed into the old pedestal rocker from her mother. She always took her sitting down time in that comfortable, old chair. She rocked herself slowly, pondering what to do.

Pictures spun through her head, mixing with the sounds of Count Basie's band coming from the kitchen. Fear and uncertainty knotted her stomach. She knew her boys had to grow up. But it was all happening too…too…well, too fast.

Sarah started to cry, her mind working back through the past hour. She wanted her sons to grow into fine men like their father, but Satch was only fifteen. And she was embarrassed but had to admit that she must have looked foolish flailing away at him so wildly and missing him in her blind rage and confusion. She also felt guilty over her flashpoint anger—that temper of hers—but she hadn't known what else to feel or do. On one hand, she wished Booker were home, but on the other, she was glad he was gone.   Today, in her husband's absence, she carried on with life as usual. She kept the boys in the house doing chores. Satch's job was to clean the stove, wash the kitchen woodwork and mop and wax the floors in the kitchen and breakfast nook. Bub's was to do his and Satch's laundry, and towels for both bathrooms.

Too bad if they resented it. She had to work sometimes when she didn't want to, and so did her husband, off up there in San Jose at an all-day pastor's meeting when he had to lead two Sunday services the next day. So why shouldn't those boys have to work sometimes when they didn't want to? The Bible said if a man didn't work, neither should he eat.

Cleanliness was one benchmark Sarah Hankerson used to judge the world. Some of the congregation thought she was "dichty," but really she was just clean, proud of her comfortable home. And she figured the pastor's wife ought to set a good example. She knew God didn't like nasty, and that made it easy for her to banish everyone and everything unclean to outer darkness. So fastidious was she that she wouldn't use the toilet or drink a cup of coffee in surroundings that failed her cleanliness test. So, naturally, she insisted that her sons clean and do other household chores like grown-ups.

Sometimes she bragged to sisters in the church,

"I'm raisin my boys to be independent. They can cook and clean good as any woman, better 'n most." Her steadfast contention was,

"I ain't gon raise up no men to be dependent on no women." And that was the end of it,

"I ain't gon raise up no men to be dependent on no women."

21

When it came to making her boys do chores and do them well, she was never more self assured. Squaring her shoulders, her hands on her plump hips, she stood as firmly as the Rock of Gilbraltar and said,

"If you're gon do a thing, then do it right." And,

"If you got time to do it over again, then you got time to do it right in the first place."

Generally, she thought they did pretty well. Sometimes when they groused about having to work, she'd snap,

"Cain't learn no younger," and Sarah would go on about her business. Sorry rascals. That part was easy, but not this.

She remembered going into the kitchen where Satch was cleaning the stove and saying, "Satch, you're gon' need to use some S.O.S. on them pipes, honey."

The boy nodded agreeably and said,

"Mom, Bub keeps mixing up my socks and underwear with his when he does laundry. Would you make him not do that? He won't pay me any attention."

She heard her youngest singing while sorting laundry in the basement and hollered down,

"Bub, git on with your job. And do it right." Bub didn't answer, but she knew he could hear her.

As Sarah started to move away, Satch called out,

"Mom, would you throw those dirty things on the floor by my bed down to Bub?"

"Lord, boy, now you gittin to be the big boss when your daddy's gone, hunh?" she chirped in what she hoped was a playful voice.

She walked into the boys' bedroom. Bracing herself with one hand on the night stand, she leaned down to pick up the bundle. As she pressed on her hand to stand up, something under the night stand caught her attention. Mildly curious, she fished out a thin, orange box, two inches square. Bold, white letters across it blared out "Trojans."

Oh, Lord! She dropped the bundle at her feet. She felt her throat constrict, her knees wobble and her eyes start to water. Oh, Lord! She breathed in fast, shallow puffs. She leaned her shoulder against the wall and felt a sharp twinge low in her abdomen. She turned the little box over and over in her hand. Her worst fear. Condoms. Trojans. Rubbers. Oh, Lord!

Sarah stood listening to the music coming from the kitchen radio and heard Satch's bumping around. She didn't think of herself as a prude, but this? Goodness! She had occasionally noticed dried moisture rings on Satch's bed sheets. Was her innocent son now a tomcat on the prowl? It was almost as if she could smell the growing maleness on him, rank, strong and insistent. She wondered if Booker had noticed it.

She recalled scenes of Satch and his friends sniggering behind their hands when the little old fast gals flounced around. She had noticed him getting taller, filling out, moving with an increasing awareness of his growing body. Those things were natural for a boy his age. But she knew what rubbers were for. Was it that Lena Welles?

She felt a thin film of sweat along her top lip. In deepest dread, she turned away from the dirty clothes on the floor and strode into the kitchen. Satch, shoeless and sockless, with his pants legs rolled up, was

23

at the sink filling the mop bucket. He made a quick move towards the radio, but stopped when he saw her face. She cleared her throat. "Carter"? she said gravely, using his given name as she usually did when she was upset with him,

"Whose are these?"

Satch looked down into her hand, and both of them stood frozen for a moment. The Nat "King" Cole Trio filled the silence,

The Buzzard took the monkey for a ride in the air.

The monkey thought that everything was on the square.

The buzzard tried to throw the monkey off his back

The monkey grabbed his neck and said, "Now listen, Jack."

Straighten up and fly right.

"Well, those are for...uh. Those...uh."

"I know what they are. I asked you whose they are," louder and more intense than she wanted to sound.

"Straighten up and fly right."

"Well, uh...I...I'm...uh ...I'm holding them for Spats, Mom."

"Don't lie to me, Carter."

He hesitated, looked away, then faced her. He paused again. The more he stalled, the stronger her feelings became. She felt her anger rising and struggled to stop it, but she hated it when he lawyered and evaded. After waiting for what seemed like forever, she slammed the box down onto the counter and stood directly in front of him. She glared up into his face,

24

"Don't you lie to me, boy!"

"Jeez, Mom. You don't have any right to be searching my room. I'm old enough now to have some privacy, and this is my private life. Just…just in case."

"Privacy? Privacy my foot," she shrieked.

Before she could even think about stopping it, as if it had its own will, her right hand, palm open, flew from her side up towards his face. It missed him and fell across her body into thin air, for he simply leaned back and turned his head slightly to the side. Without hesitation or thought, she swung it the other way, back-handed. This time, he ducked and her slap went harmlessly over his head.

She paused, stunned for a surprised moment, sucked in another breath, squared up her stance and swung again. And again, he ducked, causing her to lose her balance and almost fall. Satch reached out and caught her in his arms when she stumbled. Puffing and confused, she growled,

"Stand up here, boy, and let me slap you."

"What?"

"I said stand up and let me hit you."

"Mom..."

"Stand up and be still."

He straightened up, but started giggling. Through his laugh, he said,

"Listen to yourself, Mom. What are you saying?"

"I'm sayin..." and she stopped for a moment, hands at her sides. Through her frustration and anger, she felt her own laugh surging up her throat. Despite trying with all her might not to, she burst out laughing, leaning back against the stove for support.

Finally serious but still trying to keep from breaking up again, she planted her fists firmly on her hips, took another deep breath and declared,

I'm laughin, but I'm mighty mad at you. I'm gon tell your daddy as soon as he gets home." Her ultimate threat.

"I'm gon tell your daddy," she repeated, and turned on her heel.

"Now git your work done."

"Straighten up and fly right" trailed out of the radio as she marched up the hall to her bedroom and sat down in her rocker, stunned, still reeling from this new development.

Yes, that's what happened. She remembered it all. Remembering what had happened, however, wasn't the same thing as knowing what to do. What should she do?

The telephone rang, snapping her attention back to the present. In her mind, she could see Satch standing there on sudsy feet, looking for all the world like his father. Booker wouldn't permit his son's music in the house, but Sarah was facing a bigger, tougher problem than blues music. She rocked and listened and thought. Satch turned down the radio with Louis Jordan singing,

Let me tell you, darling

We gonna move away from here.

We won't need no iceman,

I'm gonna buy you a Frigidaire

26

When we move way out to the outskirts of town.

Sarah knew who was on the phone —Spats.

Satch, talking,

"Naw, man. I've got to help my mom in the house for awhile. Bub, too....He's doing laundry and I'm cleaning the kitchen and breakfast nook, crap like that. Yeah, I know. Probably take me a couple hours more....Yeah, I've got everything. You know I have....Maybe around two? Awright, my man. Easy now." She hated that jive talk. "Awright, my man. Easy now" echoed in her ears, infuriating her anew.

Sarah fought for long, deep breaths. A hot flash ran through her chest. She rocked and thought. Just as she asked God for more patience and a less volatile temper, so had she prayed hard--beseeching the Lord for the wisdom necessary to raise her children. Now rubbers—at fifteen. And privacy. Privacy!

She had done the best she knew how. What more could she do? What if Satch caught some nasty disease, or got some fast gal, pregnant? What then? She could just see the mean laughter and hear the wagging tongues all around town.

"Yeah, chile. R'em Hankerson's boy, that oldest one, they call him Satch, got that little old Welles gal pregnant. Yeah, chile. Whooeee!" Booker would die of shame, and she wouldn't be able to live it down.

She started crying again, giving herself over to her misery and uncertainty. Her shoulders shook and she buried her face in her hands, her sobs squeezing out of her throat. She was glad Booker wasn't home.

27

Then, and ever so slowly, an old memory insinuated its way into her consciousness, causing her tears to cease. She remembered her and Booker's marriage night. Both of them were virgins--afraid, ignorant and awkward, but passionately in love. They so wanted to do things right, but neither of them knew exactly how. She recalled the embarrassed, hasty fumbling and flailing. She remembered the sweat, the pain, the blood, the mess. As big and powerful as he was, Booker wept over his ineptness and feared he had injured her by being too rough. She wept too, comforting him and craving his body all the more.

It took them a number of failed attempts to get it right. Months passed before she experienced the pleasure and fulfillment she expected from their union. Happy, comfortable years followed, and Booker was the only man she ever had or wanted.

Sarah reached a handkerchief out of the chest of drawers near her and dried her face. She heard the music back in the kitchen go off, then a soft knock on her door. It could only be Satch.

"Mom...?" She caught her breath. Her chest felt tight. Her stomach hurt. Another knock, more insistent.

"Mom...?"

"What is it?" She heard Satch sigh outside the door.

"I'm sorry, Mom."

"I know," a slow murmur, barely audible.

"Sorry."

"I know," this time loud enough for him to hear.

His apology was without guile and answered a dozen questions racing through her brain. No, he had not had sex with any of those fast young gals, not yet anyway. Two: Times were different now. Satch was coming into his manhood, and privacy—well, being a holiness preacher's son wasn't easy. Neither was being a holiness preacher's wife. And she knew her son cared about her feelings; she heard it in his tone.

As Satch retreated down the hall, Sarah could feel the tension draining out of her body, the confusion from her mind. Her chest and stomach relaxed and she felt a pleasant slackness in her shoulders and arms. She lightly gripped the arms of her rocker and pushed with her feet, gently, slowly. A wistful smile spread over her face. Trojans! Good Lord! She rocked steadily. She loved her boy, and drew enormous pleasure from her trust in him too.

Booker would never know about the Trojans.

Farther Along

"Holy Revival," blared the huge banner tied between two light standards. Its two-foot white letters against a red background marked the entrance to a dusty parking lot in front of a large circus tent. Pulling into the lot at dusk, Satch Hankerson could see that everything was ready. The big top was stretched tight over its poles, side ropes strung to stakes in the ground. Floodlights on forty-foot poles were set at the four corners of the lot, and portable latrines stood off to one side waiting in line. Inside, the speaker's platform and the choir stand were in place. Enough wooden slat benches to seat five hundred were arranged in rows looking toward the platform, with some along each side facing the center like bleachers in a ball park.

This was to be the last night's service of the annual two-week soul-saving campaign that joined Pentecostals from all over central California. Nightly they streamed in from every direction and in all sorts of vehicles. One half of the people were black, the others mostly white but substantially sprinkled with Mexicans. All were one brand or another of holiness folks come together for the yearly blending of their styles, rhythms and tongues into a polyglot tumult of evangelical frenzy. Their fervor temporarily blotted out their innumerable fears and deprivations, their ethnic and doctrinal differences, and helped speed them on their way to that final camp meeting in the sky.

Increasingly perceived as the family chauffeur, Satch, whose full name was Alvin Carter Hankerson but who had been nicknamed after his father's baseball hero Satchel Paige, had driven his father, Reverend Booker T. Hankerson; Sarah, his mother; and his younger brother,

Frederick Harold, called "Bub," from Monterey to Gilroy where the evening's meeting would be held in a plowed field alongside Highway 101. Some of Reverend Hankerson's congregation had set up a kitchen in a smaller tent beside the big top, from which they were already selling thick, crispy chunks of fried rock cod slapped between slices of bread, boiled garlic sausages on hot dog buns, potato salad, six-inch pie crusts filled with lemon meringue or sweet potatoes, strong hot coffee, and soda pop out of chipped ice in tubs. To the worshippers, the spicy, heavy food meant more than a variety of gastric disturbances; it seemed a necessary complement to their loud, emotional service. Thus they attacked it with the same enthusiasm they did their prayers and praises. By the time the Hankerson family arrived, the cooks were sweating from the Santa Clara Valley summer and the stoves, and the pop tubs' contents had already begun helping cool down the gathering crowd.

Satch was preoccupied, silent, as he slouched his tall, broad, seventeen-year-old frame back against the seat and wheeled his father's '49 Buick northward. It was only after he had passed Prunedale and begun winding through the soft, low hills of the Coastal Range that he could pull his scattered thoughts into focus. Then he noticed how the hills refracted the fading sunlight, Indian fire scars buried under late-blooming California Poppies and blue, occasionally white, Lupin. The light made their rounded fronts bright on one side and dark on the other, and bounced in shafts off across San Benito County towards San Juan Bautista and Hollister. The hot air shimmered, heavy with smells of late summer--pungent fish fertilizer, sulfurated prunes and apricots, and, near Gilroy, the oppressive odor of field-dried garlic loaded into huge bins.

Satch should have been concentrating on his music. His father's choir, which he directed, was scheduled to sing three selections--searing gospel songs refined from his people's African past and their American present. And they resonated with the travails of white laborers and brown

31

field hands. As they had done so often in the past, the songs would at least momentarily ease the burden of dark daily lives in white kitchens and on freight loading docks. They would yet again transport these folk, distilling their suffering in this world into a glimmer of hope for a brighter day in the next. It would move them to that trance-like state in which extravagant emotion signaled both the onset and the culmination of the wrenching, convulsive rebirth into their version of salvation, which separated them from the rest of the present world.

But Satch's songs kept getting mixed up, mingling with images of Lucy Winston. Her picture and her promise lodged in his brain. She was a long-legged five-foot-five--he teased her about being "five-by-five," somewhat like the Little Jimmy Rushing song--broad hipped and buxom. Her coal black hair, freshly straightened and curled with hot irons, framed her triangular face and fell down her back in finger-sized coils. Her smooth, tawny skin was clear, and her hazel eyes, which some folks called "cat eyes," lit up her soft, pretty face. Her features would quickly arrange themselves into an open, easy smile. Her glow made Satch smile back.

She was from Salinas, twenty miles from his home in Monterey. Like Satch, Lucy was a seventeen-year-old senior in high school. Having first met the year before, they came to seek each other out at the monthly meetings of their parents' denomination or whenever there was a revival their congregations shared. They wrote letters, hers on rose-tinted and perfumed stationery with a seascape border. He also made Saturday telephone booth calls to her. They even stole a few, furtive, pecking kisses. Whenever they met and could evade the vigilant adults, Satch and Lucy, like other kids in and around the churches, exchanged significant glances, and imprinted each others' bodies through clutching "holy" hugs held a bit too long. They paired up to "cote," as the old folks called courting. Most of these adolescents were moved more by their awakening carnal impulses than any religious ones, but the pastors wanted them in their congregations anyway in hopes that redemption might suddenly fall upon them in response to someone else's fervent beseeching.

Satch liked everything about Lucy. He liked laughing and talking or just being with her. He liked to look at her (his mother said Satch thought Lucy was "pretty as a gold guinea"). Lucy thought he was handsome, and she seemed especially full and happy when they were together. They teased and chattered, talked solemnly and intensely, stood close seemingly drawn together by gravity, and pulled apart reluctantly. They never felt so alive as when they were together. That evening, her promise to meet him, and his hopes, overrode everything else as he waited for her to arrive.

Still a virgin despite the increasing itch of his desire, for quite a long time, Satch had sneaked stares at women's bodies through sheer or clinging clothes. Music sometimes gave him embarrassing erections, and when he prayed at all, he prayed his mother would overlook the spots on his bed sheets. With his buddies, he looked at pictures of naked women in magazines, and he stuck a copy of *Players* under his mattress. He joined his pals in bragging, penis-measuring talk, and he shared the masturbation guilt none of them dared admit. Lucy's face and body were superimposed on all the girls he met, for to him she came to represent the sum of femaleness.

In the end, the boy felt perplexed and deprived by his vast ignorance about women. He wondered about their bodies, so complicated, so different from his own. How did they feel to themselves--those curves and bulges, those folds and creases, those textures and surfaces? He knew the significance of, yet was awed by, their monthly bleeding, a phenomenon altogether without analogue to him. But as much as he was attracted to them, he also feared they knew more about

33

his kind than he did about theirs. The previous summer, he had tried "doing it" with Sally Smith, but her frantic clutching and bucking overwhelmed him, dampening his excitement and confounding his efforts. Later, he explained to himself that he just didn't like her enough to go all the way.

His attempts at physical discovery were further hampered by the fundamentalist protestant morality of his family. Strictures against the sins of the flesh, declared all around him in King James English, floated through his mind like words to songs.

"Thou shall not...."

"It's a sin...."

"Tis better to put thy seed into the belly of a whore...."

"Whosoever looketh upon a woman, to lust after her...."

To be sure, Satch had a lustful heart. He also grasped, though inarticulately, that his body's urgings, like those gospel songs, rose out of a base more profound and an emotional well spring more powerful than any "Thou shall not...." he had ever heard.

As Reverend Hankerson made his way to the speaker's platform and his wife decided where she wanted to sit, Satch and Bub moved around the grounds greeting other early-arriving friends. Satch mouthed helloes, shook hands and offered hugs mechanically. His mind kept wandering back to one day when he was standing out in the street in front of the church, passing a football with his cousin Spats. Old Halstead Rambeaux, sitting back against the fender of a parked car watched them and teased him about Lucy Winston.

"Yeah, Satch. I been seein you sniffin 'round George Winston's little ol gal from Salinas. That Lucy. I spec you been gittin it, too. Least-ways tryin. Ain't you?"

At sixty-four, "Bo Rambeaux," as he was called, chaperoned the choir and was friendly with the teenagers in Reverend Hankerson's flock.

He rode bikes with them, listened to their complaints about adults without tattling or judging, and teased Satch when his voice squeaked and boomed through its changes. Bo's question was more an invitation than a demand, leaving Satch free to answer as he chose, so he said playfully, wistfully,

"Maybe."

"Maybe nuthin," Rambeaux came back. "You know you is. But she a pretty thing, though."

Satch kept throwing the ball silently, but he agreed that Lucy was pretty. He thought she looked slightly Asian, something like Annette Yushima, a Japanese beauty Satch went to school with. He remembered feeling sick when the U. S. Government trucks loaded up the Yushima family and all of the other Japanese on the Monterey Peninsula and packed them off to the "Relocation Center" at Manzanar. And he was scared he'd never see them again or learn what had happened to them.

Bo stood up,

"Tell you, Satch, treat womens like folks, and they'll give you everything they got whenever you wants it." Satch's laugh interrupted him. "Don't laugh, boy. You know I done had me three wives, countin the one I got now, and I had lotsa other womens fo I got saved, so I knows what I'm talkin bout."

Seeing the Winston family's Pontiac pull off the highway under the banner brought Satch's attention back and a lump into his throat. He felt a hole in the pit of his stomach and a dry mouth when he greeted them. Lucy looked terrific but seemed tense. Satch felt scared but his mind was made up. Wordlessly, he signaled her with nods and his eyes roughly where he had parked his parents' car. He had only to get through the singing.

In that night's service, his choir was to be featured for one song just before the sermon. They would join Lucy's choir for two more songs

35

after the preacher sat down. Some other groups were to sing first, including a white husband and wife doing *"Come to the Church by the Wildwood,"* the husband repeating *"come, come, come, come,"* under his wife's melody line. Satch had heard them several times before and decided that they weren't bad, just musically simple. But he figured everyone had a right to a chance.

The young choir leader was especially nervous as he and the choir filed into the stand, and he wished he had remembered to drink a bottle of pop or some water. When they opened their song, Satch led off with a vigor that belied his feelings.

"Didn't it rain, children?" he called in his soaring tenor-baritone. Then he joined the choir to answer, *"Rain, oh, my lord."*

Satch: *"Didn't it?"*
Choir: *"Oh."*
Satch: *"Didn't it?"*
Choir: *"Oh."*
Satch: *"Didn't it?"*
All together: *"Oh, my lord, didn't it rain?"*

By the time they got through the chorus and into the first verse, the choir chanting, *"Listen to the rain, listen to the rain, listen to the rain,"* and Satch recounting the story of Noah and his ark, they were moving very, very well indeed. The excited activity of the flamboyant song allowed Satch to hide some of his agitation. Billy Jenkins' organ pushed them along, and Cora Davis' piano embroidered the ends of the singers' lines. *"Listen to the rain, yes, listen to the rain. Listen to the rain, yes, listen to the rain."*

Satch's mixed feelings remained indistinguishable. He poured his passion into his song. Without knowing it, he sang his and his listeners' dark despair and their smoldering rage, his class and racial past as well as some hopeful glimpses into his personal future. Energized, by his fear

36

of his ignorance about women, his guilt before God and his desire for his Lucy, Satch sang. Powerfully and purposefully, Satch sang. .

Between each chorus, he slid the choir up an octave or down one, putting first the men on top then the women, communicating with those quick looks and subtle gestures that comprise the private language of musicians and lovers. Each modulation pressed the singers' round tones harder against the listener's bodies; each shift thrust the choir's surprising harmonies deeper into the crowd's awareness. The organ spread out a firm foundation and the piano, sometimes teasing, sometimes pounding, promised higher peaks yet unexplored. The music rolled through the big top like a thunder storm flashing up among the swinging lights and raining down on them all. Hundreds of people--black, white and brown-- exploded into shouting and dancing praise. Old and young, male and female, they leaped and bounded, furiously pursuing spiritual fulfillment through physical exertion.

Satch and his choir filed out the side flap of the tent. Smiling and nodding, rejoicing worshipers stopped their tambourines mid-stroke to reach out to him, their Orpheus resurrected. Others waved as the choir passed by. Excited and relieved, Satch and the others smiled and waved back. He wanted them to believe his music originated in religious fervor, yet he feared they could see the carnal nature working so powerfully within him. Whatever the case, he had sung his best.

Satch broke away from the choir and worked his way through the others pairs of high school kids probably intent upon similar missions. He arrived at the car before Lucy did, so he had a few moments to gather up his nerve. He waved when he saw her coming. Even in the darkness only partly dispelled by the floodlights, he could see how her smooth stride off curved hips on top of dancer's legs quickly.brought her up in front of him.

37

More assertively than he felt even under the cover of darkness, he reached out, trying to pull her to him.

"Not here, Alvin!" She always called him by his given name, which he allowed almost no one to do.

"Little smooch!"

"Crazy boy!" giggling away her disapproval.

She gathered her robe draped over her arm, and ducking her head stepped into the Buick's backseat in one fluid motion. Surprised, yet excited by Lucy's willingness, Satch tore off his own robe, tossed it into the front seat and leaped in beside her, closing the door quickly so the dome light would go off. He blurted out,

"Made it."

"Uh-hunh," she giggled a bit more subdued than before. "You sang beautifully tonight, Alvin."

"I was thinking about us."

Unable to restrain himself any longer, he leaned awkwardly towards her and she nuzzled her face into his neck. Their lips locked together, and each ones' arms circled the other's body. They kissed so long Satch had to breathe, and he didn't keep his eyes closed the whole time like Lucy did because he wanted to see her face while they kissed. Feeling her breasts against his chest made him shiver in the summer heat

"Uuummm. You kiss good," she whispered.

"You too," he murmured, easing his hand slowly around from her back. Reflexively, she clamped her arm tightly against her side.

"No, Alvin," she said kissing him again. Still clutching each other, they slid down in the seat. Her White Shoulders cologne filled his nostrils. His head swam with disjointed images and sounds:

"Miss April, Playgirl of the Year--36-24-36." "Gilroy, garlic capitol of the world." "Your daddy says you're gonna have to marry any

38

one of these girls you get in trouble, and I agree." "Treat womens like folks...." "Oh, C.C. Rider...." "Listen to the rain, yes, listen to the rain."

Lucy shifted around on the seat.

"Raise up a minute, Alvin." Sitting up, she tossed her hair back and looked around out the windows quickly. Then she began unbuttoning the front of her blue, chemise dress. When she opened the clasp of her front-closing brassiere, Satch stared open-mouthed. Even in the deflected light filtering down from the tall poles, her full breasts were far lovelier than any magazine pictures he'd ever seen.

Uncertainly, he slid his palms up her rib cage and took as much of each one into his hands as he could hold. She sighed, drawing her shoulders back and thrusting her bosom towards him with a force that surprised him. He slowly massaged her smooth roundness.

He knew it was time for words. Should he say,

"Let's do it?" Should he ask her, "Gonna gimme some?" Should it be, "I want you?" Befuddled, he gasped, "How bout it?"

"How bout what?" Her voice in his ear sounded playful, slightly mocking. The song "Jesus, lover of my soul," floated through his mind.

"You know."

"No, Alvin. I'm not gonna do it with you," serious now. "We're not married and I don't want to get pregnant. Besides, it's a sin."

"But you promised...."

"I promised to meet you, and I've already done more than I've ever done with a boy before."

The warm, garlic-filled night pressed in on the car windows, and the distant sounds of worship inside the tent seemed synonymous with the holiness surrounding them.

"Aw, Lucy," voice flat. What to do now? "Don't you like me?" the oldest reproach of all.

39

"You know I do." Her words eased his fears a little.

"Well come on, then," too anxious , but his urgency softened her. She placed her palms against his shoulders, holding him up off her chest. Sweat ran down between his eyes. He didn't know what to do, so after a desperate moment he just squinted and let it be.

"You ever do it before?"

"Sure," he lied, looking away from her eyes.

"I never have." She sounded embarrassed, like virginity was a deformity. He thought about Halstead Rambeaux:

"Treat womens like folks." He kissed her mouth and whispered close to her face,   "I'll be careful, and I won't get you pregnant." Still holding him up, she asked,

"Do you love me, Alvin?"

"Yes." *"...lover of my soul"* went the song.

"Only me?"

"Yes."

"Will you tell?"

"No."

"I mean anyone at all?"

"No. I promise."

She wrapped her arms around his neck. Wildly, he kissed her neck, ears and face. She thrust her pelvis hard against his, groping for his wet, open mouth with hers.

Their heads were jammed against the car door on one side, and his trousered feet pushed against the other, but Satch balled up his long frame and climbed over onto Lucy. The way he fitted between her thighs taught him in a flash things about male and female bodies that all his sly looks could never reveal, things no high school health class would ever teach. The sounds of the preaching and shouting inside the big top merged with the pulse of their blood, blended with the harmony of their desire, and rang in their ears.   Their heat thickened the already warm air in the car. The smell of their sex--pungent and strong like the sea--brought them echoes of that primordial song whose rhythm and melody they were only beginning to hear. The only reality for them in that feverish moment was electric nerve endings and burning loins.

One impulse urged Satch to force the penetration of her opening; but he was afraid to do that. Before he was ready, his throbbing member pressed on her maidenhead, triggering her innate reflex to accept him. But inexperience and moisture conspired to foil them. He slipped off and lurched clumsily against her, still outside her body. Past doubt or hesitation, Lucy reached down between them and took him into her hand to guide him through her entrance.

Grasped firmly, Satch felt his surprise and confusion give way to the distant beginnings of that convulsive, eternal instant before the explosions he'd experienced only in locked bathrooms and the few other places a teenage boy could secure from intrusion. He knew he was sunk. His thick, milky spurts gushed all over the gates to the space he coveted. Unspeakably ashamed and embarrassed, Satch grabbed Lucy's narrow waist and hunched away in total abandon, too late to achieve through energy what he had lost through innocence. Lucy ground against him with quick, powerful thrusts, as intent as he upon filling the emptiness at her center. Try as they might, however, they could not consummate the desired coupling.

Perplexed and disconsolate, Satch relaxed on top of her, and Lucy ceased pumping. He lay puffing and frustrated, on a descending arc of unfulfilled passion. Lucy straightened out her legs and let her arms down. She turned away from him, silent, her chest heaving in short quakes.

"What's the matter, Lucy?"

"I'm sorry, Alvin."

41

He quietly laid his head down between her breasts. Her shudders made him wish he could weep too. If only he had known what to do. If only he hadn't been so scared. They lay quietly holding each other, their breathing becoming regular again. Gloom, like the fog shrouding the car windows and streaking down in tiny rivulets, enveloped them.

"You still love me, Alvin?"

"Yeah, Lucy, I do."

"And you're not mad?"

"Not at you, no."

"You sure you're not going to tell?"

"Yes."

"I mean no one."

"I promise."

After a long pause, she said,

"Sounds like the preacher's almost finished. We better go back inside."

"Yeah, guess so."

Their dressing seemed to take years, for their clothes stuck to their sweaty bodies. Satch's multi-layered guilt and failure made him feel exposed by the floodlights. He could hear the organ swelling up in waves, the piano frothing their crests. Hands, tambourines and bright, sparkling voices joined in a fast congregational song.

"*Power!*" the call rang out.

"*Power, lord,*" came the response.

"*Power!*"

"*Power, lord,*" again.

It was their signal to combine the choirs and go back into the stand. Instead of lifting Satch's spirits, the singing depressed him. He braced himself to ward off the stares of the piercing he eyes he feared would see everything.

42

Satch was morose, moved quickly, answered Lucy brusquely. Lucy, halting, wistful, rearranged her clothes, draped her choir robe over her arm and moved towards the tent. She shook her curls out and held her head up. He sneaked along behind her. As they walked into the brightly lit area by the entrance, Satch saw Lucy full on from the back. He exclaimed in a whisper that felt to him like a shout,

"Lucy! Lucy!" She stopped,

"What?"

"Wait! Wait!" Words tumbled out of him. "Your dress. It's got a big wet spot in back. Quick! Put on your robe!" Eyes wide, hand over her mouth, Lucy backed out of the light. Satch spoke up to the other choir members gathering before the tent flap.   "Come right ahead, folks. Line right up. Sister Lucy and I got to get our robes on." Then he backed up in front of her while she scrambled into her robe.

By the time the whole mixed choir had lined up, Satch and Lucy were ready. He stood to one side, confident and in control again. The sopranos filed in, stepping in time to the organ and piano. Then came the altos, Lucy in her proper place. Coming up beside him, she paused and smiled directly into his eyes, squeezing one of his hands in both of hers. She mouthed

"See you at next months' meeting?"

He smiled back with the greatest relief he'd felt in hours and answered,

"See you, Lucy Winston." She stepped off in time to the music, and he took his place at the end of the line singing:

Farther along,
we'll know all about it.
Farther along,
we'll understand why.
Cheer up my brother,

43

live in the sunshine.
We'll understand it all bye and bye.

Sunday Songs

Carter busied himself getting into his director's robe and making sure everything was set with the singers and their accompanists. The details absorbed his attention until the choir was seated in the loft behind the ministers. The group was to sing two songs in that morning's service--a fast, shouting number and a slow devotional in which Carter was to solo. Standing in front of the choir, his arms raised to the ready, he paused and looked at each one of them expectantly. When Billy and Cora finished the introduction, he brought down his hand, and the choir jumped into the first unison chorus:

"Come and go with me to my father's house, to my father's house.
There'll be no crying there.
There'll be no dying there.
Come and go with me to my father's house, to my father's house."

They repeated the chorus before Nell Johnson launched the first verse, Jesus' words to

his disciples:

"In my father's house,
there are many mansions.
You know if it were not true,
I would have told you so.
I go to prepare a place for you
so where I am,

45

You can be there too.
Come and go with me to my father's house, to my father's house."

The words brought Carter's mixed feelings into his face. But by then, moving back into the chorus, the choir swept the audience along to a crescendo of spiritual fervor which allowed him some momentary invisibility. The crowd clapped their hands and stomped their feet. Carter tried to compose himself in the short, busy pause between the two songs. He could see his father, the pastor, staring out over the audience, his mother looking up at him with a slightly worried expression on her face. He tried to control his mind and feelings to channel himself into his singing, but his body ached and his stomach muscles were so tight he feared losing breath support for his song. His mouth felt dry and stuck closed, and tension washed over him in waves.

Familiar with Carter's style and intent upon their joint responsibility, Billy Jenkins on the organ and Cora Davis on the piano laid down the basic chords, inviting Carter into his solo on "Blessed Assurance." Cries of expectation and encouragement--"Amen," "All right now," and "Sing it, son" --floated up to him. He scanned the face of each person nearest him in the audience, took a deep breath, and stepped forward:

"Blessed assurance, Jesus is mine."

Like his preacher father, he had a strong tenor-baritone voice, crystalline on the top and resonant on the bottom, with a slow, wide vibrato that caressed the tones, blanketing them in cozy warmth. He nibbled at the words, massaging them with his lips and tongue before taking them into his mouth. He could feel the choir swaying from side to side behind him as he gave out the second line:

"Oh, what a foretaste of glory divine."

Having started fairly softly, Carter next shoved his listeners back with a long, loud, high note that seemed able to pierce their flesh.

Fortunately, the words and melody came automatically, for his inner turmoil would have prevented his remembering them. All eyes were fixed on him, and he began settling into his confidence.

He had learned improvisation from jazz men--Bird, Dizzy, Monk and Miles--so Carter knew how to start his next moves from wherever in the chord changes he happened to stop. He leaned into the rest of the verse, his voice and will becoming one.

"I'm an heir of salvation,
purchased by God.
Filled with his spirit,
lost in his love."

At the end of the verse, Billy's organ filled the break, and Cora's piano played suggestive arpeggios over the surface of it. Together they ushered Carter into the second verse. He strode forth, wrapping his arms around the low notes and fondling the high ones, the mid-range tones hurtling out through space. In a mellow, young voice fine as a new instrument, he nudged long, rolling phrases to crests of feeling mutual to him and his listeners, but also too visceral, too dark, too boundless, to acknowledge out loud in church. And he thrust short, syncopated ones past conscious approval or disapproval into that place where the moment feels like forever, where pain and pleasure, darkness and light, sin and salvation merge.

The longer Carter sang, the easier his breathing came, the clearer his voice became. His resolution became ever firmer. He moved into the chorus of his song in full command of himself and his choir, lifting the audience to a yet higher plane of emotional experience. He called out,

"This is my story."
The choir answered.
"This is my story, this is my story."

47

Carter: *"This is my song."*
Choir: *"This is my song, this is my song."*
Carter: *"Praising my savior."*
Choir: *"Praising my savior, praising my savior."*
Carter: *"All the day long."*
Choir: *"All the day long, all the day long."*

They repeated the chorus once more and stopped. The crowd exploded into a frenzy of shouting and dancing praise. Loud and long, the people rejoiced!

When Carter took his seat, he was more relaxed than he had felt for hours, more comfortable than he had felt for weeks. Whatever the song, the story of the choir members and the congregation, Carter heard his own music. He heard the thick Russian accent of his voice and piano teacher Madam Kropov urging him to place his voice correctly, admonishing him to practice sight-reading until he could read musical scores as one reads books or magazines. He heard the sprung harmonies of Thelonious Monk and the high-low chromatics of the Four Freshmen. He heard Nat Cole loping through *"Route 66."* He heard almost none of his father's sermon, and he could see clear, blue Sunday-morning skies through the windows. After the service was over, he hung his robe neatly on a hanger and carefully placed it in the closet of the dressing room. Then he went home to struggle with his father one more time.

They were at odds over what Carter saw as his future. Billy Jenkins and Cora Davis were pressing Carter to join them and the three Williams sisters from Oakland in a touring gospel group. They planned to visit all the annual conferences of their denomination in Northern California. Then they would swing down through the San Joaquin Valley to Los Angeles, and end up in Las Vegas about two weeks before the start of school. Since they would be singing at church services, they couldn't charge admission. But the small, side collections and the "gifts" they

48

would receive would pay for most of their costs. Various saints would put them up at each stop, so it was likely that Carter would get home in late August having accumulated only two or three hundred dollars towards his fall college expenses.

His dad, Reverend Hankerson, looked like some kind of African prince picked bodily from the veldt and plopped down, full-grown, before his band of Christian believers in North-Central California. He was a powerful presence both in his church and in Seaside, the town springing up around all of them. His mind immediately penetrated to the bottom of issues, and cleared up confusion as quickly as a brisk wind scatters dry leaves. He hated verbal conflict, but when he finally entered it, he usually destroyed his opposition easily and effectively.

The Reverend was fiercely self-reliant, capable of working for days without sleep so he and his family wouldn't be totally at the mercy of a sometimes capricious church membership. His self-esteem made him inflexible in his views and sometimes arbitrary with people. His passionate faith in his fundamentalist Christianity, his foundation, was even more powerful than his confidence in his other notions. He took food to the poor in his congregation, visited hospitals and jails, and gave candy money to small children, all of whose names he knew when they trailed behind him chanting,

"Hi, Re'm Hankerson. Hi, Re'm Hankerson."

The pastor and his wife Sarah usually spent the afternoons between the Sunday morning and evening services napping over the newspapers or having their weekly in bed. Their two teenage boys alternated at kitchen clean up, then visited friends or did school work. That day, Carter's younger brother Bub did the cleaning. Sarah went into the marital bedroom to read the Sunday papers.

Carter and his father had the spacious living room to themselves. Eight-foot picture windows looked out into the manicured yard in front

49

and on one side of the house. Thick pile carpets muffled the sound of footsteps, and tasteful antique furniture symbolized the Hankerson's comfortable life. They used the living room when they had guests or held family conferences to settle things. That day, it seemed as if everyone was giving the two combatants all the space they needed for the debate which had raged for weeks.

The preacher sat straight up in his big chair. At six-feet four, he seemed taller than just about everyone, and his massive shoulders and chest loomed up over the padded arms and high back of his chair. Sprawled on the soft couch, Carter stared out of the windows at an early summer fog crawling up Maple Street past the house, nearly blotting out the two palm trees in front. It crowded in between things, blocking out the sun. The sky brooded.

"Funny place, California," Carted mused to himself. "Warm enough to grow palm trees, but so damned foggy you can't see em."

"I don't see how come you can't find some kinda work here at home like you did last summer," the minister said. "You could make good money working construction again."

"I probly could, Dad. You know I like hard physical work sometimes. The main thing about this trip, though, is the experience, not the money."

"What you mean it's not the money?" his father snapped. "You the one wants to go off to some high-priced music school. You think we find money layin around on the ground?"

"No, Dad," Carter said.

He had already been accepted at several California schools, but where he most wanted to go was to the San Francisco Conservatory of Music, the most expensive place. The Reverend wanted his son to do something "practical"--to find a good-paying summer job at home and to go to college to train in medicine or law. Maybe even business.

50

"Not only will you not make no money on this trip. You'll be gone rippin and runnin up and down the road for two months spendin money, and you'll come back home broke just before time to go to school. That ain't no good."

"I've saved $900," Carter said. "That'll go a ways, and I plan to work some during school"

Booker Hankerson knew in an illogical, but nevertheless rational way, that at the bottom of his heart, deep in his soul, his son was a musician. He most wanted to be a composer. How many black composers were there and how did they survive? The thought terrified the father.

The minister had made Carter his choir director, a boy not yet quite seventeen. But that didn't seem to be enough for Carter. Now he wanted to go gallivanting off with a bunch of wild, unmarried musicians and singers, and then enroll in that music school in San Francisco.

Only the night before, his wife had come out strongly in favor of her son in the controversy. Preparing for bed, she said,

"Booker, you got to tell Carter somethin"

"Well, Mama, that boy's got to be sensible," he answered.

"What's sensible to you don't have to be sensible to him," she came back.

"He's just stubborn."

"You mean independent? That's how we raised both of em."

"Not independent. Stubborn. He won't listen."

"Now don't go startin that, Booker," she flared. "He's your son. He's just like you--bull-necked and headstrong. Can't nobody tell either of one of you nothin."

His wife called him by his name instead of "Papa" or "Honey," and her eyes flashed when she spoke.

51

"He'll change when he gits a little older," he said, digging in. "I'll talk to him again after morning service tomorrow," he promised.

He prayed longer than usual before getting into bed, and as he pulled up the covers, Sarah flounced over onto her side, turning her back to him. He felt sad, and alone.

Carter had good reason to believe in his talent. His voracious appetite for organized sounds and rhythms had long been apparent. In the chorus at school, he sang many of the masters of European formal music. And he was learning the piano. He listened to Bing Crosby, Les Paul and Mary Ford. He chuckled at Grand Ole Opry's Saturday night twang on the radio, and sang along with Mitch Miller on the new craze, television. He'd often be discovered humming, turning his feelings into sounds, on his way to school or mowing the lawn, and he used his yard work money to buy *Downbeat Magazine* and 78 RPM records so he could hear and learn about jazz. Carter probably would have been embarrassed had anyone else known how true of his inner life the song *"Up above My Head, I Hear Music in the Air"* really was.

It was black music that captured him and formed the core of his musical sensibility--his people's mournful spirituals, blues wailed out of honky-tonk doors, jazz breaks syncopated and fluid, and the ecstatic singing of his father's choir. Its timbre and sensuality stirred him on levels untouched by much of the "classical" music he had been taught. He eavesdropped on Saturday mornings when his mother hummed and mumbled "Sweet Hour of Prayer" or "Just a Closer Walk with Thee" on her way from the front to the back of their house to get the vacuum cleaner. And when his father sang his favorite "Precious Lord, Take My Hand," before preaching on Sundays, Carter monitored and judged each rendition. His scalp tingled when the congregation rocked the walls with *"I Was Glad When They Said Unto Me, Let Us Go into the House of the Lord,"* male and female voices mingling into a palpable harmonic core

52

with high and low, bright and dark spots, filling every corner of the room at Friday night services.

Carter listened to those songs carefully and sang them enthusiastically. They echoed unknown predecessors in reverberating evocations of sub-Sahara sun, and a body life he recognized only intuitively. Their truth was of his blood, of ancient, polyrhythmic drums, of the wisdom born of bondage, of a universal life only dimly reflected on California's Monterey Peninsula in 1954.

From the start of his choir leadership, the thirty-odd mostly adult choir members accepted their teen-age director gracefully, as they knew him well, many of them for most of his life. And his musical interests and training influenced them. He insinuated more jazz elements into their singing, sliding willing dominant chords into augmented and diminished shadings the conservative elders would have choked on had anyone told them what was happening, although they enjoyed the new gospel sounds. One or two old sisters groused that the choir now sounded "bluesy and worldified." One Sunday even Pastor Hankerson acknowledged that his son's choir "kinda spruced up some old songs and made them pretty frisky." Carter did feel a bit sinful over the difference between what the choir sang and what the congregation understood. But he didn't feel unregenerate enough not to continue in the direction he had begun.

The young director worked his choir hard on fundamentals--time, tune, breathing and phrasing. He stressed the importance of complex harmonies and subtle dynamics. With Billy and Cora, Carter rearranged ensemble songs into call and response shouts, and turned up-tempo praises into slow, intense group pieces. He and his singers became a close-knit aggregation--facile and smooth, bright and full-bottomed, a little like the Basie band.

53

Their reputation spread over the region in a few months. Sunday night crowds packed the church before the choir slow-stepped in singing, *"Jesus is all the World to Me."* White people in droves materialized suddenly and vanished silently, like ghosts. And occasionally some of Carter's teachers would come to hear the choir, but they seldom discussed the music when they saw him at school.

Now, on this foggy Sunday afternoon, here they were, father and son, still locked in an untenable stalemate. They were silent for a long while. The air in the gracious room felt thick, and the minister seemed to be on one island, his son on another. They darted occasional, indirect glances at each other, but mainly they stared at the space in front of them or out the windows into the gloom.

"What you gon do about the choir?" blurted out the preacher. "You haven't been director for two years yet, and the choir's soundin better all the time. You mean you just gon up and leave em to go rag-tailin around the countryside? That sound right to you?"

Carter did in fact feel a little stinging guilt for leaving what seemed like an obligation in order to satisfy his own desires, and his father had never praised his accomplishments with the group quite so directly before. He sighed and said,

"They say Maybelle's coming back from Arkansas before the tour to wait here for Sergeant Waters to come back from overseas. She can take over then instead of when I leave for school. I mean, she was director before I was. And I can still help out some weekends when I come home."

"Naw," said his father. "I want my choir to have a regular director--somebody who's gon be here. If you leave now, that's it. I'll git somebody else to lead the choir."

Suddenly and inexplicably, Carter leaped to his feet. As if on springs of lightning, his father rose also, meeting him mid-stride, a heavy hand in the middle of his chest.

"Sit down, Satch," he roared. "You know I don't 'low no such mess in my house. What's the matter with you, Boy? I know you smellin your own stink these days, but you ain't a man yet. Long ways from it."

Embarrassed and a little scared of something he couldn't identify, Carter sank back into his seat.

"I'm your father," the preacher continued. "Don't you ever stand up to me like that again as long as you live."

After a reasonable interval, and breaking the tension following his unwise action and his father's last words, Carter slowly heaved himself up off and couch and went into the kitchen for a Coke. When he got back to the living room, he noticed his dad's somber expression and heard him speak in a hurt, hollow voice.

"I can't understand how come you got such a hair up your tail about this music school business. Sure, you got some talent, but folks ain't much willing to pay for talent nowadays. Not many musicians make a decent livin. Especially composers. And you black. You oughta be a lawyer or a doctor so you can control your own business. You should want to be independent enough not to have to rely on white people. Even if you a good music writer, you'll always be havin to go to some white man for help. That what you want?"

Carter set his empty bottle on the coffee table.

"Dad, I want a good life with nice things and all. But I need work that's more than just a job or a source of money. Like you do." He persisted, "Yes, I'll have to work with a lot of white people, and some of them will be in charge of things. That's just how things are right now.

But the music I'll make will be black, like me. Black people will buy it. I'll be independent, and I will make enough money. Just watch."

Reverend Hankerson exhaled heavily and cleared his throat. Then he rendered his judgment quickly and unambiguously.

"Satch, you can't go on no tour. You got to work here at home this summer. An if you'll go to college an study somethin' sensible, your mama and I will pay your whole way. You won't have to work or do without nothin. But we ain't gon give you a dime to go to no music school. It just don't make sense to me. You gon have to do that on your own." He sat back in his chair and crossed his legs.

No tour! No help! Dumbfounded, Carter couldn't believe his ears. After all those years of his parents' pushing him in school. All those sermons about getting to be the best at something, those admonitions to go after high goals, to be somebody. All because his father wanted something different from what Carter wanted? No help! Carter stared at his father. He stammered,

"Do…do you mean that, Dad? I mean…the part about no help?"

Another long pause. Then starting at the brow, Booker Hankerson's smooth black face broke apart, crumbled slowing like shale breaking off a mountain, and tears traced its crevices until they met under his chin. He hadn't meant to sound harsh and unconcerned about his child. He hadn't meant to come across as totally rigid. But he felt deeply that he was right, although being right also made him feel trapped. He forged ahead.

"Yes, son, I do. I think later you'll see it's best for you."

The boy was shaken by his father's tears, yet angered by his narrow-mindedness. He sat stunned for what seemed like hours, fighting off his own tears, his throat tight, his chest constricted. He, too, felt hemmed in. He sighed finally, getting to his feet, acknowledgement that he knew the discussion was over.

It required all his will power for him to retain his composure. Feeling choked and crowded in the house, he said only,

"Can I take the truck?" Reverend Hankerson blew his nose, nodded slightly and sadly watched his firstborn stride purposefully from the room.

Carter prepared to leave as quickly as he could, trying to mask his pain with haste. He tried unsuccessfully not to slam the door as he left the house. Gunning the motor of the big Dodge weapons carrier his family used on hunting and fishing trips, he noticed his mother standing in the back doorway.

"Carter, where you goin,' Baby?"

"Goin' down to start rehearsal a little early," was all he answered, glancing for an instant at his father's house poised atop its hill.

In that flash, he remembered his parents building that home when he was eight. He recalled the days and nights of hard work--the piney wood frame growing up out of the sandy ground, the plasterers running to and from their cement mixer, the shell of the house slowly filling in. Near the end, his father planted the two palms in front of the house, as if to represent the two Hankerson boys, and Carter measured the passage of time and his own growth by that of the trees. Only about six or seven feet tall, and slender, when planted, now they were over twenty feet tall, and thick.

He drove past the church into downtown Monterey and cruised Alvarado Street a couple times. Then he went on through New Monterey to Pacific Grove. The moist air coming through the truck window was bracing, and the smell of the sea brought the picture of his girl Lucy Winston into his head. Driving aimlessly along the rocky shoreline, Carter ended up at Lover's Point. He sat staring into the fog on the water and listening to the rolling waves pounding the boulders into pebbles below him. Time seemed to dissolve into the rising tide.

57

No tour! No help! He knew his father wouldn't change his mind. Neither could he. He felt betrayed. Trapped.

Carter was certain his father loved him. The Reverend acted out but seldom spoke about his affectionate feelings towards his sons, and a few times in their earlier years he raised welts on their behinds with the heavy belt that carried his hunting knife and hatchet. The boys understood their dad's acting out rather than talking about his love for them, and the kids loved him back.

Patiently, Booker Hanerson had taught them. Slowly and quietly he worked with them, repeating his hopeful mantra so many times the boys could predict when it was coming.

"I'm tryin ta raise you boys up to be men. My dad was drunk most of the time when I was a boy, so he didn't help me. But I'm tellin you boys these things so you can start from my shoulders and go up without havin' to slog through all the mud I did." Was that what had just happened between Carter and his father? Or had the pastor really wanted to control his son's life?

Carter thought back to all those Saturday afternoons when he dropped whatever he was doing and rushed to the radio to hear the Jimmy Lyons jazz broadcast for fifteen minutes. He recollected hearing every gospel singer who came to the Del Monte Gardens roller rink--Sister Rosetta Tharp and Marie Knight, the Roberta Martin Singers and the Wards; the *a capella* male quartets--the Five Blind Boys and his favorites, the tightly-controlled, dusky-voiced Pilgrim Travelers. He remembered lying about his age and sneaking into the Soldier's Club out at Fort Ord to hear Nellier Lutcher sing the blues.

Too agitated to sit still, Carter climbed down to walk along the beach under the street lights. He filled his pockets with round, smooth stones, then he hurled them as far as he could out over the surf into the soupy fog. An hour later, his arm sore and his feet and pant legs wet, Carter got back in behind the wheel of the truck

He recalled his father's putting him into the position of choir director and his deciding to drop the name "Satch." He thought some names were put onto people like poor-fitting clothes. His own middle name "Carter" felt like an appropriate name for him and who he would be.

Now, here he was. No help! His father's stand was wrong. He had no right. Carter wasn't ungrateful. He just couldn't turn back. Tears flooded his eyes, ran down his cheeks and dropped onto his chest. His anger and guilt mixed with his fears and threatened aspirations and poured out of him, adding his salt to that in the elements around him. When his watch said six-thirty, he started up the truck' motor, turned on its lights and headed for the church to tell Billy and Cora he'd be ready to leave as soon as they were

Flying White Horse

"You got to make up your mind," his father said, sitting in his favorite living-room chair and staring out the picture window into the early Tuesday evening fog welling up off Monterey Bay. "God don't want no half-way stuff. An this mess you hooked up with now, this combo or whatever you call it, ain't no good. You oughta let 'em git somebody else to play the piano."

"Baby," put in his mother from the doorway to kitchen, "don't you like playin' church music? I guess jazz is black music all right, but I ain't never heard nobody call it religious."

"Aw, Mama, this boy knows jazz ain't no religious music. Jazz is honky-tonk, low-life music and them that follow it is rough, good-timey folks. All fulla booze an dope, an every other kind of devilment. Cain't nobody play jazz an be saved. Satch knows that," the preacher ended, using Carter's childhood nickname.

Carter loved and wished to please his parents, but their religious narrowness threatened to block his musical ambitions. He was determined to become a composer. Playing jazz was only a step in that direction. So was playing piano for his dad's church choir. He exhaled a heavy breath. "I know a lot of bad things go on around jazz clubs and that some musicians get all messed up with drugs and stuff."

"You got that right," broke in his dad, "a lot of em."

"I know all that," Carter continued, "but the fact that some people make mistakes and do bad things doesn't mean that everyone has to. I can play jazz and learn what I need to learn from it to be a good composer without becoming a dope head or a bum. I'm me, not just some piano player."

"Well, you cain't be hangin aroun no honky-tonks, playin jazz or nothin else and play music in my church." There was the nub, flat out. He had to choose playing with and for the choir or with his band. Period. Simple as that.

Carter made an oblique challenge. "Dad, you've got some folks claiming to be saints who do a whole lot worse things than play jazz music. I mean, look at Bessie Miles. And Beepo James. Both of them are as much out of the church as they are in. Bessie's got eight children by nobody knows exactly who, and Beepo's lucky if he can sober up in time to go to church on Sundays. And you don't put them out of the church. So why would you put me out for playing music you don't like?"

"What's wrong wit you, boy? I'm the pastor of that church, and I know who's right an who ain't. I don't need you to tell me that," from the preacher.

"But what are you gonna do about em?" Satch persisted.

Pretty hot himself by now, Rev. Hankerson took up the challenge,

"Since you so smart, what do you think I should do? Throw em out and have em wander out into the world and be los for sure or keep em around the church, even if they slippin and slidin and fallin and gettin up? Long as they close aroun, there's at leas a chance the Lord might touch em. So what would you do?"

Carter sighed again and mumbled,

"I don't know for sure what I'd do."

"I guess you don't," Booker Hankerson snapped back. He went on,"Besides, you cain't judge a church or a religion by people like Bessie and Beepo. Neither one a them got good sense. Everybody know that. An it takes good sense to serve the Lord, good sense. God holds people

61

responsible for what they know an what they can do, like the men the master gave different talents to in the Bible--the one that got ten talents was responsible for ten, the one that got two was responsible for two. Now you, you got plenty sense an you gittin a good education. Me an yo mama never did git no good education like you gittin. So you responsible for yo own talents, not Bessie Mileses' or Beepo Jameses'. God wants servants with clean hearts and upright spirits. An good sense."

"But doesn't it also say that God is merciful and looks into every man's heart and judges that, not just what appears on the outside?" his son argued back.

Carter knew he was vulnerable arguing biblical interpretation with his dad. But he believed he was right.

The Preacher began, "Course God is merciful an looks on the heart, but..."and the telephone rang.

Relieved, Carter leaped up and went to the telephone table.

"It's for you, Dad," he called back into the living room. Then he headed down the long hallway for the bathroom.

He returned through the kitchen just in time to hear Rev. Hankerson tell his wife, "It's about Jewel Johnson. She's in the mental hospital up at Agnews."

"Oh, my Lord," Sarah exclaimed.

"You remember how she used to scratch and talk to herself," he continued."They say she got so bad she couldn't hardly keep still. Then yesterday, she set herself on fire. Seem like she did it on purpose."

"Was she hurt bad?" Carter asked in alarm.

"Naw. She run out inta the yard burnin. Brotha and Sista Hollis was drivin by an saw her. They put out the fire and rushed her to the hospital. The doctors sent her up to Agnews in a ambulance this mornin. Guess I better go see her tomorra."

Carter draped his long frame over a chair, his tension from the argument somewhat diverted by shock and sadness over the tragedy to one of his favorite people. Listlessly, he turned on the evening television news, but he stared past the set out the window into the fog, thinking about Jewel Johnson. She was so devout, so holy. Back when her husband Herm and her young son Michael got killed in the car wreck, church folk said she slipped some. About two years later, when she had a baby out of wedlock, they thought Jewel came loose. Now she had gone completely over the edge. Hadn't she had enough trouble already? What kind of God did all of those people worship anyway?

Jewel was a missionary in Reverend Hankerson's Pentecostal denomination. She said God called her to the missionary field when she was just a fourteen-year-old girl. Like he called men to preach. She kept a home in Sacramento, but traveled all over California running revivals at holiness churches. She went to big buildings in San Francisco, Oakland and Los Angeles. She went to storefronts in Modesto and Salinas. People came in droves to hear her speak, to be healed or saved. She was Aimee Semple McPherson all over again, only black.

When they were being formal, churchfolk called her "Sister Johnson," but the rest of the time, she was "Sis" Johnson or "Jewel." "Chile, you shoulda heard "Sis" at Re'm William's church las week!" or "Man, time Jewel got through singin an prayin, two folks had done throwed down their crutches and started shoutin for joy," they'd say. She had power, yet she was humble. And she belonged to them, their own towering, heroic figure.

In addition to being gospel mighty, Sis Johnson was a phenomenal physical beauty. She was nearly six feet tall, lean but curvy, and charcoal black. The whites of her eyes and her even teeth contrasted sharply with her smooth, dark skin. Her high forehead and cheek bones,

63

her nose and mouth, were so perfectly formed that her face and head looked sculpted out of obsidian. She embodied her name.

Carter Hankerson always looked at Jewel Johnson with wonder. She was not too much older than he was, probably not more than thirty-six, but she seemed far beyond him. She fairly radiated power and passion. She was so consecrated to her work, so fervent, yet so warm and direct, and so beautiful, that she confused him. Her devotion fascinated him. Her beauty drew him.

Whenever she stayed at his parents' house to run revivals at the church, Carter felt excited, warm and full. "The spirit tells me Brotha Carter's gonna be a preacher. He don't know it yet, but I believe God's gonna lead him to do a great work, praise the Lord," she said one evening after dinner back when he was seventeen. Then she fixed her gaze on him and smiled a smile that seemed meant only for him, one he thought suggested some vague, unspoken secret between them. Carter's brown skin hid his blush, and his breathing sped up.

Now, trying to picture Jewel's condition, Carter remembered instead a particular night back when he was fifteen or sixteen and experienced his most powerful contact with her ministry and with her. In a joint meeting of several congregations at Reverend Highsmith's church in Redwood City, Sis Johnson was the featured speaker. Standing beside a table on the floor down in front of the pulpit, her red robe flowing around her like a mantle of anointment, she preached into the sea of black faces in front of her. Her sweet soprano voice, strong and clear, seemed to shower down from the ceiling upon everyone in the room.

Jewel clasped her hands in front of her full bosom, her red robe set off by a white collar that the glaring overhead lights made sparkle against her black skin. She tossed her head and opened calmly,

"Saints, my subject this evenin is 'Be sure your sins will find you out.' See, the Bible says man looketh on the outward appearance, but

64

God looketh on the heart. God looketh on the heart. God sees your heart. Don't matter how big or little you are. You can have all that this world's got--money, clothes, cars, people doin whatever you tell em to do--you can have everything. But if you ain't right with God, he knows cause God sees your heart. Doctors an' lawyers, politicians an' bankers, an' all other kinds of high people, they'll cheat an steal jes so they can get rich. They can look like they so right, so kind, but lotsa times they'll take advantage of you, take your money an not do what they supposed to do. You all know I'm tellin the truth. You know white people." Amens and laughter came to back to her. Having heard her many times before, Carter recognized Jewel's race-tinged, edgy gospel.

She strode back and forth in front of her table, picking up momentum, as stories, examples and lessons flowed from her in a rush. She expounded upon her theme for over half an hour. Then moving towards her close, she said,

"Evil is in men's hearts. Women's too. Everybody's. Sista, you honey," pointing to a front-row saint in the corner with a Bible on her lap. "Read me Mark the seventh chapter startin at the twenty-first verse." Jewel knew the scriptures chapter and verse, often stringing together long strands of readings and quotations.

Proud of being called upon, the woman read from her Bible,

"For from within, out of the hearts of men, proceed evil thoughts, adulteries, fornications, murders. Thefts, covetousness, wickedness, deceit, lasciviousness, and evil eye, blasphemy, pride, foolishness: All these things come from within, and define the man."

"That's enough, darlin. Close your book. I don't think I need to say nothin else. Do you? That's the word of the Lord, children. Your sins will find you out."

The amens quieted a little, the laughs disappeared. "All them sins Sista jes read about, they all in the heart. I can't see em sometimes. Can't

65

nobody else see em sometimes either. But God looks in our hearts. The wages of sin is death, but the gift of God is eternal life through Jesus Christ our Lord. That's Romans 6 and 23. The wages of sin is death. Not might be. Is death. But, hallelujah, the gift of God is eternal life. An that gift, saints, that eternal life is only in Jesus. Ain't you glad you know Jesus? Ain't you glad? Ain't you glad he died for you? Don't you love him for it? Praise God, we don't have to take death wages. We can have the gift of life through Christ Jesus."

She let out a high, loud whoop and stood for a long moment, her body twisting and jerking spasmodically, her right hand raised high, her head down, speaking in tongues. The congregation erupted. Shouts and cries of joy rang out over Sis Johnson's voice, drowning her out. People clapped their hands. Some stood up and waved their arms in jubilation. The woman beside Carter rocked from side to side in her seat, hypnotized by the beautiful, spirit-filled, woman preacher.

Then Jewel stood still. She raised her arms above her shoulders and spread them out in front of her, the palms of her hands upwards and open in a gesture of welcome.   "Oooh, church. We don't know when he's comin. This might be my last night here with you. It might be yours. It might be all of ours. The world might end before mornin. We jes don't know. But we   know that when judgment day comes, people will run and weep and tear themselves.

"Don't let that be you. Even if you're a good person but haven't given your heart to the Lord. Even if you don't commit any what you might call big sins, jes what seems like little ones, but you don't know Jesus. Don't matter who you are or what you know, you need to be saved. You need to know Jesus. Cause Revelations tells us if your name isn't written in the book of life, you'll be cast into the fire. Don't let that be you. Don't let that be you. Your sins will find you out."

She began singing, and the congregation joined in, *"You're gonna need somebody on your bond...Way in the midnight, when death comes creepin in the room...You're gonna need somebody on your bond."*

While the singing continued, Jewel stepped to the side of the aisle and beckoned to the audience.

"Come, children. Come pray with us. God'll save you. He'll forgive all those little sins nobody else don't know about. He'll give you relief; he'll bear your burdens; he'll lift up your heart. Come, let us pray with you."

The congregation kept on singing softly, *"You're gonna need somebody on your bond...way in the midnight, when death comes creepin in the room, you're gonna need somebody on your bond."*

Caught by Jewel's sermon, Carter thought about his sins and visualized himself prostrate before God's wrath. His head felt light. His mouth felt dry and his palms moist. His throat felt tight. His breath came in short gasps. He feared he might die and be sent straight to the pit of fire and brimstone that very night. Perhaps at that very moment. Sweat trickled off his scalp and down his neck. It ran from his armpits down his sides. He was terrified. Simultaneously, he felt another sensation, a generalized carnal attraction to the tall, handsome evangelist stirring his nascent manhood.

Suddenly, almost without his knowing it, borne up by the strong gospel and the powerful singing, and drawn by her spiritual power and her physical beauty, Carter rose from his seat and joined the line of supplicants shuffling down the aisle towards the altar and Sis Johnson. Her voice soared over them, bringing them to her. His fear weighed his shoulders down. His now redoubled guilt bowed his head. Tears filled his eyes. Yet the warmth in his loins persisted.

The singing rolled on, *"You're gonna need somebody on your bond."*

When she saw Carter approaching, the missionary smiled her special smile at him and said,

"Praise God! Pastor Hankerson's son. Sing, children. God's gonna work a wonder. Call on the Lord, Brother Carter, call on him loud." She grasped his right hand in hers, placed her left hand on his forehead and began to pray,

"Lord God, touch this young man. Save his soul tonight, Father. Set him on the righteous path."

Carter stood mute, a pillar like Lot's wife.

Suddenly, he felt her soft lips on his cheek. Her left hand on his back eased him along to keep the line moving. At that moment, he became so flustered that his feelings almost overwhelmed him. Any religious impulses he might have experienced left him. By the time he struggled back to his seat, he was certain that he hadn't been saved, but his skin tingled where she had kissed him.

Now, just a few years later, Carter sat in his parent's living room, ignoring the TV set, feeling afraid and sorry for Jewel Johnson. That Redwood City night now long and far behind him, Jewel was in the mental hospital. Out of her mind. He had not seen her in several years, though he still cared about her. Would God have mercy on her, his fallen servant, or would he be the hard, wrathful deity Carter's father preached about?

Carter decided to go along to visit her the next day. Sitting in the back seat of his parents' Cadillac as his father wound up Highway 101 towards the state hospital, Carter thought about his dilemma, about the choir, about his band, about Jewel. Ten miles south of San Jose, the Hankersons drove past the spot among the vast prune and almond orchards where Jewel's husband and son, Herm and Michael, had been killed. Herm had fallen asleep while driving from Salinas to San Jose,

68

from one of her revivals to another. He had run head-on into a semi truck.

"I cain't never go past here without thinkin about poor Brotha Johnson and his boy," Sarah Hankerson murmured. "I jes pray that the Lord'll hold his hand over us and protect us on the highways."

"Only the Lord can do it," from her husband.

The church people said Jewel hadn't seemed much effected by the untimely deaths of her mate and child. She simply said, "God's will be done." And after the funerals, she returned to her revival in San Jose. She also began furiously campaigning for souls all over California. She threw herself into the work with no heed to her own fatigue or wellness. She ran meetings in the Bay Area, in Los Angeles and San Diego, over in the San Joaquin and Sacramento Valleys, everywhere.

Then people started noticing that she began to change. She took on some girlish traits, acting immature--giggling and ducking her head shyly when she talked, and she started mumbling to herself what seemed like prayers or songs. Two years later, after she delivered her own still-born child, a girl, wrapped her in a shawl and slept beside her, people were shocked. No one had even been able to tell she was pregnant, perhaps because she wore her trademark red robe so much. While everyone wanted to know, no one knew, or could even guess, who the father was. And Jewel wasn't telling.

After her brief lying in and the infant's funeral, Jewel began to scratch herself. First her arms, then her breasts, neck and face. Finally, all over. "Jewel's in trouble,"
church members all around the state said, and they vowed to pray harder for her. God seemed not to have answered their prayers because now she was insane, lost among her fantasies and fears, locked away in an asylum.

69

Once at the Agnews State Hospital, Rev. Hankerson drove slowly down the long, tree-lined drive to the central building. While waiting for his father to locate Jewel inside, Carter wondered aloud to his mother,

"What'll she be like?"

"I don't know," she answered, "but somehow, seems like to me none a this woulda happened if she'd of been a man."

"What do you mean?"

"Jes that men have it easier. People ain't so hard on them. They give em more money, an forgive em for stuff quicker 'n they do a woman. You remember Re'm Benbow down in Fresno had two children by the same unmarried girl in his church and didn't nobody do nothing. He's still the pastor there. An you know Bishop Jenkins is crazy as a bedbug." Carter nodded and chuckled.

They waited for what seemed a long time. People passed the car, sometimes waving or smiling.

"All these people look normal to me," Carter murmured. "I don't know who's crazy and who's not."

"Me too," his mother replied.

Suddenly, Sarah Hankerson said,

"There they are," pointing to her husband pushing Sis Johnson, strapped into a wheelchair, around the corner of one of the smaller buildings towards the car. Even in a drab, light green hospital dress, with her arms in sleeves bound around her torso and tied in back, Jewel looked handsome to Carter. Her shoeless feet were encased in gauze, and her legs were wrapped in bandages up to the knees. But her hair was neatly combed, her smile was bright and fresh, and her head bobbed as she talked animatedly to the minister. His expression was somber.

Mother and son scrambled out of the car. Jewel rushed on, seeming not to pause for a breath.

70

"Lord Jesus! Sister Sarah! It's so sweet a y'all to come see about poor Jewel in this evil place. Y'all the only ones been here. God bless you. An Brotha Carter, my favorite pastor's son. I prophesied that God's gonna do a great work through this young man. How you doin, baby?" Her eyes darted back and forth to each one of them, sparkling, wary, wild.

"Fine, We're doin' good," Carter and his mother answered in unison. "You doin all right, Sis?" asked Sarah Hankerson.

"Aw yeah, I'm fine, Sista Hankerson. It's jest these ole doctors and nurses they got here. They think I'm crazy, but I ain't crazy, y'all. Really. They said I set myself on fire, but I didn't. I prayed to the Lord to git rid a the bugs--mites or somethin--on me. Little tiny ones you couldn't hardly see. They was all over my body. The spirit set the hem of my garments to burnin an the bugs went to runnin an leapin every which away. I mean they was leavin this body, praise God. The Lord was workin a wonder." Her voice trailed off and her eyes shifted back and forth from one of them to the other.

"God bless you," breathed the minister softly.

Jewel rattled on,

"I jest wish I didn't have all these ole belts an straps all over me." She twisted and turned against the leather harness binding her into the wheelchair.

"Act like I'm liable to go somewhere. Chile, Jewel ain't goin nowhere. She ain't got nowhere to go."

She started crying, but she didn't stop talking, sometimes to the Hankersons, sometimes to herself, sometimes to her dead baby.

"Don't cry, baby, Mommy's right here. Aww, poor thing, you ain't breathin. Lord, help your servant's chile. Pray, y'all. Call on God. I know he's able, and the devil's a lie."

Sarah Hankerson wept softly into her handkerchief. Carter's throat felt

71

tight and dry, as it had on that long-ago night when he met Jewel at the altar. The Reverend looked solemn.

Sis's head drooped forward towards her breast as if she were dozing or praying silently. The pastor and his wife looked at each other for a moment, then he stepped forward, saying,

"Would you like us to pray with you, Sista Johnson? You know the Lord is our rock in a time of trouble, a shelter in the time of storm." She perked up and smiled at him, that special smile that Carter so cherished.

"I'd appreciate that, Pastor."

The minister and his wife inched closer to Jewel's chair. Their son backed away and sat down on a bench nearby. Booker Hankerson placed his left hand on her brow and raised his right to heaven. Sarah gently rubbed the back of Jewel's neck and the tops of her shoulders. Jewel closed her eyes. The prayer was long and quiet, almost a whisper. People passing by lowered their voices and moved in a wide arc around them.

When the prayer ended, Sis's face brightened, and her talking started in again. "Lord, I'm so glad y'all came to see Jewel. Y'all the only ones been here. I ain't gonna be here long. The savior's gonna come for me. The spirit's done already told me that. But 'fore y'all leave, I'm gonna tell y'all somethin'. Somethin' I ain't told nobody else. Y'all come up close. You, too, Brotha Carter." Beckoning them with her head to come closer to her chair.

Nervously, the Hankersons eased up to her. She leaned forward confidentially after glancing quickly around.

"Everybody keeps on askin me who my baby Sadie's daddy was, but I haven't told em. I'm gonna tell y'all. If anybody asks you who baby Sadie's daddy was, tell em I said he was a flyin white horse." Then she shreiked, so suddenly and so loudly that the Hankersons jumped back in alarm.

"A flyin white horse," Jewel screamed, convulsed with laughter. Then she writhed and wriggled around in the chair, laughing, crying and trying to scratch herself.   Carter broke into a run for the door of the central building. In what seemed like an instant, two male attendants and a female nurse rushed down the walkway. Carter followed right behind them.

Jewel struggled, and thrashed, and screamed, and wept, and swore, all so violently that she nearly tipped over the wheelchair. She screeched curses that embarrassed Carter to hear in front of his mother, and she called the staff people awful names. Her guttural grunts and growls sounded vaguely like her, but more they seemed torn from some other source at once untamed and yet familiar, so deep inside her that it was clearly beyond the veneer of civilization, past the relevance of religion. That quality and character of her cries chilled the listeners and nullified concepts like prayer, sin or salvation.

The Hankerson family stood shocked.   The hospital staff restrained Jewel as quickly as possible and whisked her away into the maw of the big building, leaving a calm so dense that she seemed never to have actually been there. A silent, serene, surreal moment surrounded everything and everyone.

Carter drove towards home for several miles before anyone said anything. He momentarily stopped the radio's tuning knob at a station playing the Modern Jazz Quartet. When his father cleared his throat and glared in his direction, Carter turned off the radio. He wasn't sure exactly how or why, but seeing Jewel Johnson had cleared things up for him. He'd never argue religion or music with his parents again.

His mother broke the silence from the back seat,

"Lord, that po girl. Los her husband and two babies. Now she done los her mind.   Seem like, sometimes, when bad things start

73

happenin to ya, they jes go from bad to worse. But I guess God knows how much we can bear. Have mercy, Jesus."

"The Lord's the only one can help her now," from the minister.

"I jes feel like some a this wouldn'ta happened if she had of been a man," Sarah repeated.

"Well, man or woman, she sho does seem pitiful. Sista Johnson was a good woman an a fine missionary. Now here she is, outa her mind. An unless God makes a way, her soul gon be los. An thas' a shame."

"Ya see, son," he spoke towards Carter beside him, "this is what I was tryin to tell ya yesterday. Anybody cain't understand right an wrong cain't understand the gospel an salvation. It takes sense to be saved. Can you see that now?"

Carter hesitated a moment before answering. Then he said,

"Yeah, I guess so," and stared straight ahead of him down the highway.

Where is Home?

Here I am heading off alone to Ann Arbor, into the mid-western "heartland," to the bottom of Michigan's Upper Peninsula, to the University of Michigan School of Music. Maybe I pushed her too hard. Maybe she wanted to settle back into the warm, fuzzy L.A. Jewish scene she left for school, more than she wanted to risk inter-racial life with a black dude arrogant enough to think he could become an important composer. Maybe I was just moved more by my gonads than my brain cells.

Tiffany's a talented enough singer to have made a place for herself at the University, and my fellowship is big enough for us to have lived on until she could take hold there. Maybe she's right, that letters, phone calls and occasional holiday visits can maintain what we have, well enough for us to take a little more time deciding where we're headed. I'm not anxious to risk that, especially in view of how we left each other at the end of the summer in Modesto. The pictures of that last Sunday in the park on the Tuolomne seem to stick right in the middle of my forehead, and the feelings they bring up make my stomach hurt.

The big plane's rising and banking sharply to turn east shows me the Golden Gate, all the bridges and the Bay Area, in a manner greatly different from what a person sees on the ground. And it means I really am going away, a long way. Any way....

I didn't really plan to do what I did that day on the river. I was just lying there in the tall grass staring at Tiffany's tits. Just staring, and remembering, and feeling bad. Next thing I knew, I had jumped into the god-damned river.

Her name was Tiffany Mossberg, and she was from Los Angeles. She was five-six, what my mother called "chunky" and nearly as strong as I was. Soccer and surfing had done for her what swimming, basketball and tennis had done for me. Her skin was olive and her short hair was bronzy brown, but her eyes were the thing. They were huge, light green almonds that danced and sparkled. I couldn't stop gawking at them. Her full, red lips looked moist all the time.

We were both working at the California State Honors Music Camp held at Modesto Junior College. That small-town J.C. had the best auditorium and rehearsal facilities in Central California, better even than most of those in San Francisco. This was one of those in-between jobs young professional music aspirants took on their way somewhere else. Tiffany taught voice, and I was the first black student composer and orchestra conductor the camp ever had. Dr. Andre Williams, my composition professor at the San Francisco Conservatory of Music, made sure I understood that - the creep- that old stuff about "being a credit to my race," and "blazing a trail for others to follow." Even so, he gave me a stellar recommendation, and I got the job.

Just two days earlier, we had given our session-ending concert. Tiffany had sung first, and then ushered her tenor-baritones with unpredictable voices and her one-note contraltos through their performances. I had dragged rather than led my perpetually flat brass and woodwind players through their paces. Then we had sent them home to small valley towns like Ripon, Gustine and Manteca bearing evaluation letters from the camp's director, Dr. Henry Marshall. We had drafted the notes, which he gladly signed. "Dear Mr. and Mrs. Blank," they read, "I am pleased to inform you that your Sadie has earned my highest recommendation to the Conservatory...." Or, "Dear Mr. and Mrs. Blank, after working with your Johnny for this entire summer, I judge that he is not yet ready…Perhaps as he matures…."

Ahead was Monday, when she would climb into her already loaded Ford Victoria coupe and head south to Los Angeles and what she called "the next step." I would aim my Chevy two-door towards Monterey, where I'd visit with my parents for a week before catching a plane for Ann Arbor and graduate school. Everyone--my San Francisco faculty, my parents, and the University of Michigan graduate school of music (which was putting up the money)--thought a Ph.D. would get me off to a better start in my professional career than a B.A. I thought "everyone" was probably right, but I didn't want to leave my princess with the amazing green eyes and big, firm boobs. So I was feeling bad at the Tuolumne River Park that Sunday afternoon. Even before all that river shit dropped right into the middle of everything.

I was remembering the night before and the other nights like it all summer. Puffs and pants, groans and grunts, welling up over the dim candle light in my room. Body odors making the warm air close and musky before she'd open her second-story window for a breeze. Sticky limbs sated and sprawled on wet sheets before sleep. I adored her spongy breasts rising off her chest like volcanoes, her furry belly, her firm thighs, her startling green eyes that stopped me in my tracks. She said she loved my hands, so strong on the piano yet so gentle on her body, my voice rumbling in her ears. Jesus! We must have generated enough electricity to light up the whole San Joaquin Valley. She startled me back to the present by asking,

"Want a beer?"

"Not yet."

"Anything else you want?"

"Yep."

"What?"

77

"To nuzzle your boobies."

"Insatiable beast," she grinned.

"Rawweeeer," I growled, leaping up and pushing her roughly over onto the grass beside me. I climbed on top of her and tore playfully at her halter top, swearing to rip it off and dive into her bosom right there in front of God and everybody.

"Carter, you wild-man son of a bitch," she screeched before laughing uncontrollably into a pant. When I rolled over onto my back, I didn't even bother trying to hide the erection that made my bathing suit stick out in front. She laid her head on my chest, tugging gently at the short hairs above my belly button. We were twenty-one, painfully passionate about each other, and terrified about our future.

The midday heat was killing--at least 105--and the people in the park by the Tuolumne River huddled in what little islands of shade the scattered trees provided as shelter against the scorching sun. Everyone in the park that day was after the same thing we were--being as still and getting as cool as possible in that blazing August.

Near us on the grassy knoll several families of Mexicans listened to the San Francisco Giants baseball game on a portable radio. They laughed and talked to each other in Spanish, and the men cheered, *"Si, si! Bueno!"* when I mock-wrestled Tiffany to the ground. Most of the other folks in close range, mainly white except for what looked like a black church group, firmly dug in at a safe distance from the rushing summer river, pretended not to see us.

Tiffany and I sat up, straightened out our blanket and popped a cold Lucky Lager out of the ice chest. We rearranged our sunglasses and surveyed our domain in the most sedate manner that our youth and our suffering allowed. Despite our resistance, we felt ourselves being pulled into conversation, as if by the force of the river itself. And we tried so hard not to talk. I mean, really talk. I was the one who opened it up.

78

"Tif, why dontcha come try it at Michigan for a semester? Nothing big's gonna happen in L.A. until after the first of the year anyway."

"What do you mean, nothing big? I can work all that holiday stuff--those parties and shows. It's good money and I can meet some people. Make some contacts."

"But Jesus," I pressed. "They have some really good faculty back there. Might even get Leontyne Price this year. You heard that just like I did."

She was ready for me.

"What you mean is there are lots of good people for you to work with--Wilson, Morris, Chernisky--lord only knows who. Michigan will be good for you but not for me. Right now I need exposure, not more schooling." I knew she was right and wanted to stop, but I couldn't turn it loose. So I went all the way to the place we were trying so hard to avoid.

"What the hell's gonna happen to us?"

She turned slightly towards me and laid her head on my shoulder. I was breathing fast and sweating in the heat, but I could feel her tears plopping onto my bare skin. Then she sat up straight, shook her hair back and wiped those, almost Asian, green eyes. She looked at me with such sadness that I had to turn away to keep from letting her see my own full eyes. After a moment, she said softly and evenly,

"Carter, you know I gotta go home. You've always known. I don't want to go to graduate school now. My family wants me in L.A., and I want to be there." She paused, then went on, "Hon, if our thing is as right as it seems to us at this moment, your blackness, my Jewishness, whatever, we won't be able to stop it, and neither will anybody else. You'll come racing out to L.A., hard-on in hand, or I'll fly crotch-first into Ann Arbor, and that'll be that." She gave my shoulder a hard shove and I fell over onto the blanket. How could she be so sure? Wasn't she afraid at all?

"Hey, watch my beer," was all I could manage, trying to see if the Mexican guys were still watching us.

She was right. We both knew all along that we were having a summer "thing." And "the future" seemed like an enormous black hole then, and now even in an airplane at 27,000 feet. That was all before I learned how I felt about her. God! How we laughed. How we talked, really talked. How easily we made good mutual decisions. How cozy and comfortable our loving was. That was all before "the future," some of which I guess is now.

Tiffany Mossberg! Damn! It didn't seem like it, but I'd known her for three years, and she'd always been that way--quick, direct if not brash, and final. I met her at one of those Conservatory parties during my first year in the City. My steady girl Lucy Winston had stood me up. Said she couldn't make it from Salinas up to San Francisco for the year-end bash. I didn't really believe her, but it was just one more in that series of missed connections and poorly understood conversations that led to our final break. My response was to get roaring drunk and dance the night away to Dixieland jazz. And to meet Tiffany Mossberg.

I had just lurched back into the room where people were dancing, trying to compose myself for another assault on the floor. The very good band was playing *"I've Got a Home in Indiana"* louder and hotter than I ever heard it before. Suddenly, there she was, standing at my left shoulder. She wasn't conventionally beautiful. She was stocky and strong looking, a "sweat sock" as people called female athletes, a sort of feminine term for "jock." On the street, I'd probably have passed her without a second glance. But the closer I looked at her dark, green-eyed face with a mocking smile just beneath the surface of her skin, the more powerfully her sensuality and her jaunty edge drew me towards her.

"You're Carter Hankerson," she said. "I heard your first-year recital. Pretty good." I glanced down at her and answered,

"Right," in the coolest, most drawn out, disinterested way I could.

"And you are?" I asked.

"Tiffany Mossberg." Then more standing and listening to the music.

When the band dropped into *"I Got a Right to Sing the Blues,"* I said to her, "Well, are we gonna dance, or what?"

"Let's hear it for 'or what,'" she said, burrowing her face into my chest and backing onto the dance floor. She stopped and said,

Carter's a last name. How come a cat like you ends up with a name like that?"

"Dunno," I lied softly into her hair, though I knew full well the story of my parent's choice of my name. Then I came back,

"Tiffany's a lamp, isn't it?" She grinned, I grinned, and we locked together in the dance. We flowed into the music, our young bodies picking up the rhythm, playing out the melodies hour after hour.

Once when the band finished a set and took a break, C.J., (Cornwallis Jones), the hip jazz drummer sitting in with group, nodded to me. He was a cat I had jammed with a few times before he split to try his luck in New York. He sidled up to me at the bar and said,

"Hey, my man, a fifth of Black Jack says ain't nothin' happenin' with the Jewish American Princess tonight."

C.J. was like that, always signifying or putting somebody up to something.

"You're on, Ace," I shot back over my shoulder as I moved to meet Tiffany coming back from the restroom.

When I went by his pad on Cole Street near Golden Gate Park to collect my whiskey the next week, C.J. said, "Man, I knew I was done for when I saw that chick look at you on her way from the can."

"I know what you mean, Man. But this girl's really nice," I replied.

Tiffany and I saw each other a few more times around the school or the city, went through all the stuff about my studies in composition and hers in voice, her Jewish family in L.A. and my black one in Monterey, and then slowly, steadily drifted apart. She was the first white girl I slept with. Early on, I was pretty uncomfortable with her. I was nothing like my cousin Smitty who seemed drawn towards white women only. I didn't plan on getting involved with a white girl. I knew my folks, especially my mom, would have a fit. And I didn't believe all those tales about black men and Jewish women either. It just happened.

Three years later, we stumbled unexpectedly upon each other again, standing in the lobby of the auditorium at Modesto Junior College getting ready to work as teaching assistants in summer music camp. I was a little flustered by seeing her and didn't know exactly what to do or say. I got out,

"What's happenin?"

"God," she sighed squeezing my hands, "at least there'll be someone here that I know. Maybe I'll survive the summer in this hick town after all."

Boom! We were together again, giggling, talking, touching each other. In hushed voices, we quickly settled all the necessary details-- graduating from the Conservatory, what our jobs in Modesto were, what we planned to do next, where we were staying for the summer. We fooled around and carried on all the way through the program-opening performance by the faculty string quartet. To this day, I can't remember what they played, but I do remember how people in the audience stared and frowned in our direction. After agreeing to have dinner and see a movie together that night, Tiffany and I went about our work.

We ate Chinese in a greasy little place on McHenry Avenue, then drove her car out Highway 99 to a drive-in theater south of town. Crossing the bridge over the Tuolumne, I could see the rapid, powerful river under the bridge lights. I could hear its song, simultaneously sinister and serene as it went by, boulders rumbling the bass line, small rocks and pebbles the treble. It seemed to be hurrying, racing towards the sea a hundred miles away.

We watched Gene Kelly and Natalie Wood plod their way through *"Marjorie Morningstar"* and listened to the river a football field away. She pushed me away when I tried to kiss or fondle her. That confused me because it was so different from how she had been with me earlier in the day, so I was glad when the lights mounted high on telephone poles came on. We drove out.

Tiffany parked her Ford in the carport beside the house where she had an upstairs apartment. I was feeling a little rejected by then, but I reached for her again anyway. She slid over against me and kissed me back so strong and so long that my ears rang. Then she abruptly pushed me away again and started getting out of the car.

"Where you goin'?" I asked.

"To put in my diaphragm, where do you think?" she said, fumbling for her keys.

That day and night began the summer for us. We worked all day in air-conditioned buildings, out of the valley heat, but long after sundown and far into the warm, fragrant nights, we walked through the comfortable neighborhoods around the college. We played early-morning tennis before classes started, each winning about as often as the other. We swam in the college's pool or the river on Saturdays. We ate fresh-picked apricots and peaches for breakfast at her place and mine. We got drunk on gin and tonics and laughed arrogantly at our students and the other teachers. We talked until daybreak--about race, religion, sex, politics, war, work, money, marriage, family, what it would be like working in our careers.

We made music, too. Some Sundays, I played the piano for her rehearsals. God-damn she had a good voice--a mezzo soprano that filled space, pressed in on your body and seemed to come at you from three levels up and three down. When she sang, her face looked soft, her magical eyes fixed on some spot on the ceiling out in front of her, and her voice seemed to come from some place other than her muscular body. After her work, we'd improvise Jackie Cain and Roy Kral scat duets-- *"Mountain Greenery," "A Foggy Day in London Town,"* tunes like that. What fun!

Some days she'd see me on the campus and ask,

"Have you done any writing this week?" I originally planned to spend most of my off time that summer working on several pieces I took with me to Modesto. But that was before Tiffany. She seemed to know when my answer was a lie, and she'd bore into my chest and ask,

"What the hell are you here for, to do music or me?"

My usual, joking answer was, "Now that you put it that way...."

Those nights, I'd write because I really did want to finish at least one piece before the summer was over.

We knew our parents and friends back home would never quite understand us, and we sometimes tried to explain away our racial and cultural differences. Mixed-race couples simply weren't all that common in 1956, in California. My blackness and her Jewishness supplied a feeling tone, like a warm blanket on a winter night, wrapping us in a kind of cocoon. We both knew we were very different from most of the people surrounding us. I talked about white people and she talked about goyim as if the terms had no relation to us or our lives. We never mentioned each other in phone calls to our families. We laughed and

84

loved our way to August, mainly seeing, hearing and thinking only about each other. Suddenly we were facing separation, maybe forever. On that last Sunday picnic, our past together and the prospect of a future apart floated through my mind, taking my attention away from the heat, the sounds of the river and people talking and playing all around us. Long, long ago that was.

Damn! How long have I been asleep? My watch says nearly two hours. Far past the big, western mountains, we're now sailing miles above a yellow, green and brown patchwork of grain fields like a checker board or quilt. Fields periodically separated by hedgerow strings of trees or streams meandering crookedly through them. Middle America. There it is--bread basket of the world. I hope I didn't snore. I've got dry mouth. I'll get a can of pop from a stewardess. Where was I beside here? In the park by the river, yeah.

Looking back on it from here, I really don't know which I noticed first, people running and hollering or Tiffany's cry,

"Carter, look!" The terror in her grip on my arm snapped my head around towards the river. The Mexicans above us were shouting and pointing. People were scrambling every which way and lining up along the river bank. I jumped up, still trying to figure out what in hell was going on. Then I saw it--two dark heads bobbing and tumbling down the river towards us.

"Go call the fire department or the cops for help!" I barked at Tiffany, gesturing towards the row of telephone booths near the concession stand by the road. Then I sprinted for the water. My left flip-flop hung up between my toes and I had to stop to kick it off, the other one too. Then I kept running. The staccato cries of the crowd gathering on the river bank came at me through the shimmering heat.

"Look! Help! Somebody git 'em! Oh, my God!"

By the time I worked my way through the milling, screaming mob to the bank, the heads had disappeared. People were still yelling,

"Git a boat! Call the cops! I got a rope!"

But no one was in the water.

Without slowing down, I swore over my shoulder, "Sons of bitches," and dashed, rather than dived into the water.

No one went with me, or followed me.

The icy water, contrasted with the summer heat, shocked me into realizing fully how dangerous the situation was. As I laid out into a crawl stroke, I saw the heads bob up again twenty or thirty yards ahead of me in the river. That's when I started hearing in my head a stern, firm voice rehearsing the drills I learned in lifesaving courses:

"Use your strongest stroke. Keep your head up so you can see the victim. Don't fight the current; use it. Protect yourself at all times."

The strong, snow-swollen current threw me down into a whirlpool, and for a moment I almost panicked as I spun and thrashed, completely out of control. When I managed to scissor kick back to the water's surface, choking and spluttering, I couldn't see the heads. But I struck out for where I saw them last. As I floated and swam downstream, still alone, the shouts from the shore became one with the roar of the river. The water was swift and deep. My lifesaving instructor's voice droned on in my head, *"You can't save anyone if you drown yourself."*

Then I saw them ten yards ahead of me. Two Mexican boys, I thought, about eight or ten years old. One was struggling, his head clear out of the water. The other, much worse off, was slumped over, slightly submerged, not flailing. He seemed to be clinging to the active one and being swept along by the river. I knew then that I'd at least reach them. Kicking as hard as I could to gain speed and stroking as strong as I could to control myself against the current, I approached them from the back.

86

I tried to sweep them to me with one arm. I missed and they drifted a few feet away.

I lunged forward, gathered the struggling child to me and reached over him after the other one who had begun to slip away when I touched the first one. I tried to shout to him to grab my hand, but the other boy's thrashing, the river's rush and his condition kept him from hearing me. The river was sweeping all of us downstream, and I was getting tired. Holding tightly to the boy I had in my right arm, twice, three times, I reached for the submerged one with my left hand, trying to grab an arm, a leg, his hair, any part of him I could get a good hold on.

I missed every time. When I tried once more and saw more than felt his hair slip away from my stiff, clutching fingers, I knew I had lost him. I had failed. He was gone.

My mind flashed back to how Eddie Benjamin drowned on one of my dad's church picnics at Pacheco Lake, and how people said I'd have saved him if I had been there instead of away at college.

"In a multiple drowning," my water safety instructor's voice rang *in my ears, "don't risk everyone by trying to save one more."* Holding tight to the one child I had, I reluctantly turned towards shore.

I swam at an angle towards the bank, keeping the frightened boy's head up out of the water. God-damn, I was cold and tired. My blood pounding, my breath coming in painful gasps from my burning chest, my left arm wrapped over the boy's left shoulder and around his belly, I kicked with my legs and stroked with my other arm. My body seemed locked in slow motion, like a sleepwalker's.

My mind raced. Sensations and ideas ran together. That was the first time I'd seen a person die, and I was shocked by how simple and quick it was. Just a brief flurry, then nothing. My stomach ached. I felt guilty. Sad. Angry. I noticed a sharp pain just below my right knee, but I kept swimming.

As I got out of the river's main stream into the shallower, smoother water, I was able to separate the shouts of the people on shore from the sounds of the river.

"Hoorayy! Got 'im! Somebody help 'im! Where's the other one?" I could hear the child whimpering in Spanish, *"Santa Maria...."*

I was still the only rescuer in the water.

When my feet slammed hard against the river-bed sand, I staggered up to my feet, lifting the small boy in my arms. People with ropes and tree limbs ran into the water to meet us. They yelled,

"Go back! Git the other one! Hurry!" Wearily and wordlessly, I shoved my way past them without even looking at them, deposited the crying child on the ground and stumbled up towards my car and my girl. People smiled and waved at me, and some reached out to touch me as I went. I couldn't see or hear Tiffany, but off in the distance, I could hear sirens coming towards us. Then she appeared from somewhere and threw our blanket around my shoulders. I was bruised and scraped, and I hurt all over, but the ache I felt inside was unspeakable.

I leaned gasping against the car, the blanket still wrapped around me, and watched the people rushing, milling and streaming out of the park. Ignoring the hot metal, I slid down the side of the car and laid on the ground shivering and weeping under the blanket and the merciless San Joaquin Valley sun.

After a long while, when my crying and shaking subsided a little, Tiffany put her arm around my shoulders. She said,

"C'mon, Hon. Time for us to go home."

Sitting up, I answered, "Where the hell is home?"

Shame bitter as gall rose up into my throat as soon as I asked that mean question. I felt so guilty, so angry, so desolate. Dumb me! Damn me!

She asked me to fly down and see her once before I headed east. And she forgave me, saying,

"Oh, Carter, you big schnook. You did hurt me, and I was really mad about that. But I believed you loved me, and when I thought about where we were and what you'd just been through, my pain and anger went away."

We made love in my hotel room, walked on the beach at Santa Monica, and talked long into the night before she dropped me off and went back to her folks' place.

We relied on long letters and longer phone conversations before all the rigamarole of my leaving. We ended our last conversation with her saying,

"Will I see you at Christmas when you come out to see your family and get your car?"

"Nothing could stop me," I replied.

Now here I am circling Detroit in an airplane. It's only 6:00 o'clock, so I'll eat and then catch the van for Ann Arbor. I understand that Detroit's a good city, but it sure looks different from the West and the Bay Area. No hills and not right at the water's edge. Ann Arbor's out in the suburbs, and smaller.

I have to do something about housing, shopping, banking and all of that crap before my first advisory conference with Anton Chernisky. I've heard he can be an arrogant, Russian son of a bitch, but I've seen those before. Oh, well....I'll probably be able to make my way here somehow, turn this place into home. At least until the Christmas break.

A Good Provider

Sarah was hot that Saturday morning, hotter than she'd been in a long while. With absolutely no warning, not a single solitary word, her husband had gone out and bought a new Cadillac, and yet he wouldn't let her buy new furniture for the living room. Antique, French Provincial. That's what she wanted and had hinted about for two years. It was partly the money, and Lord knows they had already spent plenty on Christmas things, but it was more Booker's attitude and insensitivity that rankled her. He expected her to want a big, ostentatious car as much as he did. He couldn't seem to understand how much she wanted to make their house look nice to show how good their life was.

She poured herself another cup of coffee and flounced back down into her chair at the breakfast table. Alone and pouting, she stared through the windows of the breakfast room, and let her eyes wander over the sand dunes and out towards Monterey Bay. Here it was just two weeks before Christmas--they had the tree up and everything--and for her it might as well have been no holiday seasonat all. Sarah's Christmas spirit was gone.

Booker was outside showing their oldest son, Carter, the family's newest, most expensive toy. Carter was home from college in San Francisco for a weekend visit. He'd be back again for Christmas, and she wondered if her youngest, Bub, would get a Christmas leave from the Navy, or have to stay in San Diego. She thought about the gifts she'd bought her sons, and smiled to herself, confident that her husband would

90

"surprise" her yet again this year with still another pair of shoes and a handbag. The thought added to her depression.

"Lawd, Lawd, Lawd," she muttered, getting up to haul the breakfast dishes into the kitchen.

Sarah Hankerson was a short, cream-colored woman. At forty, though tending slightly to plumpness, her figure was still firm and soft in the right places, and her curled hair framed her round face, which was accentuated by her little pug nose. Her pert movements and alert eyes showed her vivacity. Her husband said she was feisty "like a little Fice pup," and while the church members felt her warmth and friendliness, they also liked to think of her as spunky.

Her bad mood lifted some as she busied herself putting away the food and washing the dishes, humming distractedly under her breath as she worked. Carter came in behind her, wrapped his arms around her waist, picked her up and swung her around.

"Wanta drive over to Salinas in the new car with your oedipal son at the wheel?"

"Put me down, you big ox," she shrieked playfully, twisting her shoulders around and kicking her feet in the air.

"I don't wanta go nowhere, and I don't care about no new car neither." A slight pause, then, "What's oedipal?"

" In the Greek myth, Oedipus was the man who killed his father and married his mother. What do you think of that?"

"Well, if that's all they got time to teach you at that high-priced school up there in the City, I'm glad I didn't go to college. Thought you was supposed to be studyin music anyway? Besides, if there's any killin gets done around here, I'll be the one doin it, an without no help."

He set her down affectionately and kissed her neck, both of them laughing at her joke.

91

"Sure you don't want to go? he pressed. "Might help you feel better."

"Yes, I'm sure, an no, I don't wanta go, feel better or not."

Carter was tall and muscular like his father, a good husband for some woman some day she thought. A rush of love for her boys momentarily erased her anger. She mused about the times she'd curl up on the foot of one of their twin beds and have long conversations with them, talking frankly and directly, like friends. Often, she'd conclude by saying,

"What you decide to do for a livin's up to you. I jes hope you guys'll be like your daddy when you get to be men. One thing everybody's always said about him is that he has been a good provider, never has made me an y'all want for nothin."

It was eleven o'clock. Sarah had already put the ham hocks on to boil and was picking the mustard leaves off their long stems to be added to the pot later, when her husband came into the kitchen.

"Mama, do you know where I can find Speedie's choke chain an rope?"
he asked. "I thought we'd drive down through Carmel Valley and up over Los Laureles Grade to Salinas. Might see a flock of pigeons or a covey of quail, an the dog could retrieve em for us."

"Naw," she snapped up at him. "I don't hunt so I don't mess with no huntin stuff."

"I jes figured we'd put the dog's cage in the trunk…," he trailed off, heading back out into the hallway.

Sarah hesitated a moment, relented a bit. Then she called out after her husband,

"Look down in the basement in that room with all that other huntin an fishin junk. It might be there."

92

It didn't seem odd to Sarah that Booker would shoot a shotgun out of a brand new Cadillac or haul his dog in the trunk of it. That's how he was about hunting and fishing. Typically, when he was finished with some piece of equipment or a tool, he'd just throw it down anywhere, only occasionally hitting what he called his "gear stack." He didn't feel towards his possessions like she did towards hers. Didn't dote on them or take pains caring for them.

After twenty-two years, Sarah was still in love with Booker Hankerson. She thought his powerful, six-foot-four-inch body handsome, his bearing dignified. She liked riding beside him in the car, shopping next to him in the grocery story, lying entwined with him in bed. All her married life she had resented her parents' attitude towards her man.

"A big, rusty, black field hand," they'd called him. Hadn't wanted him to have their dainty, fair-skinned girl. But he had become a man of substance, and now pastored the largest black congregation on the Monterey Peninsula.

Despite how generous the members were to them, Booker and Sarah struggled to be financially independent of the church. He fixed up and sold old houses and cars to make extra money, and she guarded their meager reserves carefully, adding to them from house money whenever she could. At last, they saved enough to leave the parsonage and build their own house on a hill in a growing neighborhood quite a distance from the church. Their comfortable home had an air of stability about it, was a symbol of their hard, honest effort. Unfortunately, she thought, her confidence in Booker and their success just added to his stubbornness, a source of some of their marital problems.

They shared most decisions, but the Hankersons nearly always disagreed about money. However broke they were, Booker never wanted Sarah to work outside their home. As their boys grew, she wanted to do

93

day work for a little extra change like some of the other young women in his growing membership were doing. When Booker spotted her list of potential employers, he pitched a fit that lasted for a week.

"You can't go," he finally proclaimed. "My wife don't do no day work for white folks. She cleans up her own house." Case closed.

She understood his race pride and his determination to supply his family's needs, but even so, she felt more dominated than comforted. True, she sometimes playfully called him her "lord and master," but everyone knew that was a joke. She gave in on the day work issue because the possibility of her hiring out seemed to hurt him so, to make him feel so small, and he was, after all, a good provider.

Their biggest money arguments were usually about what to do with money once they got hold of some of it. Sarah liked to save it, and felt safe having a few dollars around for what she called "an emergency." To Booker, having money meant spending it for things that not having it denied him. She laughed out loud remembering all the times her husband spent money to save it, such as buying those five cases of tuna fish because they were such a good deal when he didn't even eat tuna.

In honesty, Sarah reckoned she was just as bad as Booker in her own way. She'd hoard money in little nooks all around the house--$25 in a small, brown envelope tucked into a book, $50 tied in a hankie and dropped into a vase. Then she'd forget where she had hidden her treasures, and she'd scramble around, embarrassed. Sometimes, she'd stumble upon one of her secrets in a box or under a stack of linen without remembering when she put it there. Sarah knew she didn't need to hide money, but having it squirreled away made her feel secure.

She got out the flour, shortening and yeast to start Parker House rolls and crusts for custard pies, Carter's favorites. She could hear her son running his electric shaver in the back bathroom and Booker

94

rummaging around down in the basement—leaving a mess for her to clean up, she thought resentfully.

She thought of the nine thousand dollars her parents left her. It wasn't all that much when you came right down to it, but it was enough to make her feel free to do a few of those special little things she wanted to do for herself and her family. It was also just enough money to set Booker on edge. He would sometimes refer snidely to "her money, her inheritance." Then they'd fight--Sarah flaring up, Booker stomping angrily out the door to go down into his shop under the garage and tinker with his outdoor gear.

The kitchen clock said twelve-forty-five. The rolls were set on the stove to rise, and the pie shells were baking in the oven. The rich, spicy aroma of the now boiling greens floated through the house, promising a tasty dinner. Sarah dried her hands on a towel, and as she rubbed in Jergen's lotion, she went into the den to look out the window at her husband and son gawking at the new car.

This was his first Cadillac. But from the time when he was a poor, farm boy, he dreamed of having one, "the best car made in America," he had said repeatedly. Sarah watched how he beamed his pride of ownership, how like a conqueror he strutted around the long machine. Booker called it "a '58 Sedan de Ville" and said it had the biggest engine and the most modern conveniences General Motors had yet invented. Sarah expected it to burn a lot of gas.

She didn't begrudge him the car, but how could her husband be so callous towards her desires? To his mind, being able to own and maintain a new Cadillac showed that he was in control of his life, that he could command respect. When some of the other preachers they knew bought them, Booker had held out, saying he wouldn't buy a Cadillac until he had a garage to park it in. Now he had both castle and carriage.

95

"Lawd, Lawd, Lawd," she murmured aloud to herself again, and, still disgruntled, made her way to the basement to pick up the things she knew her husband had strewn from one end of the room to the other.

When she got back upstairs, father and son were in the living room fooling around with the Christmas tree lights, wires and tools spread out on the carpet. The minister seemed jumpy. The son looked impatient.

"Thought y'all was in such a all-fired hurry to go to Salinas, or huntin, or wherever you goin?" Sarah charged from the living room doorway.

Booker answered, "Jes thought we'd put the new switch in this light cord fore we went. Won't take but a little bit."

"I'm ready to go now," Carter said. "I want to drive the new 'chine and try to pick up a few quail."

"Won't be long." His dad promised. Sarah couldn't understand why Booker was dawdling so.

"Don't make me wait dinner, now," she warned.

"Yeah. Yeah, we goin." Booker began to gather up the lights. She started down the hall towards the kitchen.

Just then the doorbell chimed. Sarah turned and opened the door. She saw a big, gray van parked in front of the house. The sign on its side said "W & J Sloane, Fine Furnishings." A white man in blue overalls tipped his cap to her and smiled,

"Here's your furniture. From Sloane's." Another man waited in the truck.

Confused, she said, "We didn't order..." and stopped, not knowing what to say next.

Carter came to the door and spoke to the man on the porch.
"Hi."

A little uncertain, the man said, "Reverend Booker T. Hankerson live here? We drove up from L. A. with a load the dispatcher said had to get here today."

Embarrassed, Sarah spoke up, "Yes, this is the Hankerson house. Please come in.

"Where's your daddy, Carter?"   "I don't know, but I'll get him."

He met his father coming up out of the basement.

"Went down to put the tools away. Guess we can fix that cord when we come back," Booker mumbled sheepishly. "What's goin on here?" feigning ignorance.

"A couple guys are here with some furniture," his son told him.

"Oh, Oh, okay. Where you want em to put this stuff, Mama?" he asked, working his way past his wife in the hallway. "It's your livin room suite."

"But I thought....you said ... when did you?" she stammered, glancing quickly at Carter. The long awkward pause seemed to rise up from the floor, like a ground fog.

"Las week. Well...you. wanted it so bad, an it bein Christmas an all. I jes figured.... Well, anyway, it's here now," her husband finally blurted out.

It was the very French Provincial she wanted. First, there were two sofas--long and low in a cream-colored fabric richly brocaded with red roses and gold leaf. Their straight backs were trimmed in warm brown wood that swept under the narrow, padded arm rests and down to hand-carved legs. And the sofas were matched by two occasional chairs. There were two other side chairs and a soft, rose ottoman that matched them. Then there was a square, mahogany coffee table with a marble top and a tall, rectangular one that matched it. Last, there was a cherry wood writing table with a soft, comfortable chair for Sarah.

The truckers puffed and sweated the pieces, one by one, into the living room. Carter helped. Booker shepherded,

"Watch the walls. Don't scratch it. Wait. Wait. There, that's it," he called, rushing back and forth from the front door into the living room.

Sarah sat down in the dining room doorway, her recent anger gone, her eyes brimming, her thoughts confused.

When the truckers and the van full of her old furniture finally left, the house was filled with a sudden quiet. The spacious, square living room absorbed all the new pieces and took on an air of gracious ease. It looked far better than Sarah had imagined possible. Alternately laughing and crying, she wandered from piece to piece, marveling at its detail and stroking it lovingly. As she passed by Carter, she'd give him a squeeze, and she'd hug Booker and give him pecks of kisses as she went. Over and over she said,

"It's beautiful, Papa. Don't you think so, Carter ?"

"Well, I was gon see to it that you had that furniture if it meant sellin the car and walkin." Carter watched and grinned, enjoying his parents' love for and pleasure in each other.

Sarah kept repeating,

"Lawd, Lawd, Lawd. It sure is beautiful!" Looking up at the Christmas tree, she said, wistfully, "I sure hope my baby gets to come home for Christmas so we can all be together and enjoy our new furniture." She paused briefly. "And our new car," she mumbled through a wan smile at her husband.

Booker got up quickly.

"C'mon, son. If we goin to Salinas, we better git goin." Carter scrambled to his feet. Going by Sarah who was caressing one of her new tables, Booker hesitated, bent down and grabbed her thigh under her dress, saying,

"See ya' later, hot stuff."

"Quit it, Booker," she snapped in mock anger, slapping at his hand. "Think you smart, don't ya?" she hollered as he went laughing down the hall.

Sarah sat down at her writing table, rubbing its smooth surface. She was delighted with her new furniture, and Booker's surprise was complete and exciting. As her husband and son went out the back door, she heard Booker tell Carter,

"There's things go on tween a man and his wife can't nobody else understan." Carter replied,

"Uh-hunh."

Tears rolled slowly down her cheeks and met under her chin.

Glorious

Her name was Gloria--Gloria Jackson-- but her older sister Josie said their mother, Elsie, called her "Glorious" from the day she was born. Elsie thought her newest baby "glowed" from birth. Her straight sandy hair, her light skin and her hazel eyes all seemed to be nearly the same, translucent tan color. She seemed lit from under her skin in the same way some of those New Zealand Maoris give off a kind of orange light.

A few months had passed since Carter Hankerson had seen her, though she was the widow of his closest friend "Doc" Jackson. Parking his Chevy SUV in front of the Jackson house on Maple Street just below Noche Buena Avenue, Carter rolled up all his windows against the fog bank rolling in off Monterey Bay, cold and brooding. Then he looked up at what he always thought of as "the house that Doc built." It sat a few blocks down the hill from the Hankerson family home, just off Broadway, around the corner from the church Carter's father had founded, the Community Pentecostal Church (CPC to long-time Seaside residents). Glorious was a member there. Doc's house looked firm and strong, though it needed a paint job, and the lawn and flower beds looked a little tired.

He rang the bell.

"Oh, my goodness, come on in Satch," Glorious hollered, throwing her arms around his neck. One of the few people he still allowed to call him by his childhood nickname, Glorious ran on. "I thought you were one of those triflin girls of mine comin back here to get somethin they'd left."

100

Sweeping her off her feet into his arms and swinging her around, Carter growled into her neck, "How you doin, Glorious?"

Once her feet settled back onto the floor, she answered a little breathlessly, "I feel like killin those girls of mine, but beside that I'm OK."

Glorious was five-feet-three and one forty-five. Not fat, but a short, square block of a person with thick legs and ankles. Her physical being gave off an air of firmness and stolidity. Carter's mother, Sarah, called her "bodily."

Despite her substantial look, there was a certain tentativeness about Glorious. She scurried about in short, quick steps, her head bowed and tilted slightly forward as if to escape a threat or ward off a blow. She still came across as stable, reliable. She saw and spoke the truth however quietly.

Glorious's family home was in Warren, Ohio, a tough, hard-scrabble, industrial town in the mining and manufacturing northeastern region of that state. Her white father was a floor supervisor in a factory that produced sheet metal for Michigan's automobile industry. Glorious was the next-to-youngest of seven children. Her light-skinned African American mother died giving birth to her last child, a male infant who also died. Seizing that day, the father deserted everyone, never to be heard from again. Glorious and her surviving siblings spent several years in a white church's orphanage on the outskirts of Warren. During that period, three of the remaining six children also died--one drowned in Lake Erie, one was killed in a car wreck and one overdosed on heroin. As Carter learned more and more of her story over the years, he often thought of her as representing a paraphrase of the line from Ray Charles's song, *"If it wasn't for bad luck, [Glorious] wouldn't have had no luck at all."*

Glorious came to Seaside when she was seventeen to live with her sister, Josie, whose husband James was sent to the Coast Guard station in

101

New Monterey. Josie was seven years older than Glorious and helped guide her through graduation from Monterey High School. Then Glorious went to a program at Monterey Peninsula College and became a Licensed Practical Nurse. She took care of a rich, white invalid in Carmel. A number of church folk were a little surprised when Doc Jackson married the quiet, unassuming young woman, both of them thirty-five.

"When did you get here?" she asked Carter.

"Day before yesterday. We came down for Mother Wilson's funeral, which I thought was really nice. I never would have heard the last of it if I hadn't showed up."

"I couldn't make the service but I'm glad it was nice," she said. "And I know what some of these Seaside folks would have said if you hadn't been there."

"You know how that old lady was about me. Mom used to say it was a good thing I look so much like my dad because if she had ever gotten half a chance, Sally Wilson would have stolen me and claimed I was hers."

"I know that's the truth."

"Remember how Mom and Dad used to make me spend time with her? I used to wish she had had just one kid of her own."

"I remember how she used to make over you when you was growin up, buyin you stuff and always askin you to play and sing for her in church."

"Lord yes."

"Did Claudia and the kids come with you?"

"Oh yeah. Little Booker's got one of his ear aches, so Claudia's sticking close to him. She stayed at Mom's place with him, but told me to tell you hello. Michael's up there in the den playing one of those damned shoot-em-up video games and Anna's hiding in a corner texting everyone she knows."

Carter thought about how tight Glorious's body felt to him when he picked her up in his ritual way of greeting her. She seemed as if she were holding in some sort of physical pain. He was her closest friend, as he had been with her husband. Like he was a close older brother, rather than a friend more than ten years her junior.

She picked up the conversation,

"I haven't see your kids since your dad's funeral except for a minute once when you guys were here and that was months ago. How old are they now?"

"Michael's fifteen, Anna's twelve and Booker's seven."

Glorious shook her head, "My Lord, time passes fast."

"Damn! It's crazy, Glo. We're getting into that teenage stuff. All Michael wants to do is drive the car or play those awful video games and Anna's getting moodier and meaner every day."

"Well, you've got one that thinks he knows more than you do about everything, one that hates the sight of you and all humans who aren't about to start their periods and one accident." They both laughed loud, knowing laughs.

"You got that right."

She went on,

"You just got to hold on and hope they grow up sooner than later like mine seemed to do."

"I heard that." They both laughed again, nodding their agreement. Carter noticed again that his friend seemed to be distracted, playing a little behind the beat. Glorious spoke up as if she had just startled awake,

"Look at me, makin the professor stand up in the front door like an Avon lady! Lord have mercy! You got time for a cup of coffee or tea? I like hot tea when it's foggy and chilly outside like it is today."

"I'll take coffee if you have it made."

103

"Just take a minute. C'mon in the kitchen so we can sit at the table. Watch out for all that mess on the floor. It's part of what's left of my clock collection. I just haven't been able to make myself clean it up yet."

Carter stepped carefully over and around parts and pieces of ornate, little gingerbread clocks scattered around on the floor. Figures, plastic pieces, springs and wheels seemed to be everywhere.

Getting settled at the kitchen table, Carter noticed that all five ornamental clocks Glorious had so carefully protected and so proudly displayed were gone. So was the wooden wall rack that held them. She called her clock collecting "saving time." Doc gave her the first one as a belated wedding present, and she bought the others at different times and places over the years. Glancing around the kitchen and breakfast room, Carter asked,

"Where are the kids?"

"The two oldest ones are at school up at Noche Buena. The two little ones are down for their naps."

"What ages are they now?"

"Well, lemme see. Raylene, that's Cheri's oldest, is seven, and Lena's one, Bertha, is five. Then Cheri's Ronnie is four and Doris is two."

Besides Cheri, who Carter figured must have been around twenty-six, and Lena, about twenty-three, Doc and Glorious had produced two other children. Their first-born was Donnie Ray, Jr, called "Baby Doc," who would have been getting on towards thirty had he not been killed falling down a stairwell at school when he was nine. Their youngest, Jenelle, would have been about twenty had she not been killed in a car wreck the night she graduated from Seaside High School, more Ray Charles kind of luck.

Carter sipped his coffee and connected Glorious's comment about being angry at the girls and the broken clocks. He cleared his throat,

"So, Glorious, tell me about the clocks."

"Well, Satch, it's long, sad story if you want to know the truth. You remember Doc was the one that got me started in on clocks. He gave me the first one in the first year we was married. You remember the one that had that kind of gold lace around it and rang that nice little chime every our?"

He nodded.

The telephone rang, and Glorious got up from the table to answer it out in the little hallway that ran back to the bedrooms upstairs and down. While she was gone, Carter's thoughts ran back over the years of his friendship with the Jackson couple, and his special relationship with Glorious's late husband. Doc and Glorious had both been thirty when Carter was eighteen, and some church members wondered how Doc and Carter had become such good friends, given their age difference. Carter was the Pastor's kid and all, but were they "funny" or what? Doc explained it quickly and easily, by saying,

"H-h-h-he's smarter than all them other young knuckle heads up there round the church put together."

Donnie Ray Jackson came from Mobile, Alabama to Seaside when the United States Army sent him to Fort Ord on his way to Korea. He claimed people who knew him turned the first two letters of his given and middle names into "DR," then "Doc," the name he had been called for nearly as long as he could remember. Doc was very dark, and, like Carter, over six feet tall, maybe six-feet two or six-feet three. But unlike the muscular Carter, Doc was lanky bordering on skinny. Even so, he was very strong and coordinated. When they first met, they spent hours and hours shooting at the hoop mounted on the Hankerson garage or winning

105

pocket change in two-on-two pickup games on the Noche Buena School playground.

The two young men became nearly inseparable. Doc and Carter helped each other work on their cars. They pried Abalone off the rocks along the rocky shores of Monterey Bay and caught flavorful Sand Dabs out of the surf. They ran around Northern California from the Bay Area to Los Angeles for church musicals. While Carter became his father's choir director, Doc never professed religion or joined the church, but he loved the music and mingling with the young church crowd. He liked to tease and play, but he was a person of substance. Sarah Hankerson acted as if Doc were her third son.

Doc had a slight stutter which sometimes momentarily blocked his ability to speak. But once he got past the first word or two, he usually spoke rapidly and clearly,

"S-S-S-Satch, you got any bread?" And he had a big, rollicking "Huh-huh-huh" of a laugh. Stupid people thought his speech impediment meant he was mentally handicapped too, but Doc was bright and creative. He was also a smart, strong, hard worker.

About three years after his discharge from the service, early one Saturday morning on a weekend when Carter was home from college in San Francisco, Doc called the Hankerson house.

"S-S-Satch," he said, "m-m-m-m-meet me down at the M-M-McDonald's on F-F-Fremont and M-M-Maple." Carter didn't hesitate, but he noticed that his buddy was obviously nervous. Doc was already there when Carter arrived.

Carter had barely ordered his coffee and sat down at the table when Doc burst out, "S-S-S-Satch, I'm-I'm-I'm gonna marry that sandy little Glorious. I c-c-can't git her outa my mind, so I guess I'm gonna have to m-m-m-marry her." Carter knew Doc and Glorious had been

106

seeing each other for a little while, but he had no idea it was this serious.

"Have you asked her?" Carter came back.

"N-N-Not yet. I n-n-need you to go with me up to J-J-Josie and James's house and talk-talk-talk to them while I ask her."

"Damn, Doc," Carter protested. "You should do that by yourself."

"I can't, god-dammit. Would I ask you if I didn't n-n-need you?" Carter gave in,

"OK."

Of course, Glorious accepted Doc's proposal while Carter sat out in the kitchen drinking coffee with Josie and James. Both of them beamed and smiled as they came in and told Glorious's family and their best friend what by then was no news. They also insisted that Carter be the best man. Six months later, in sharp, rented tuxedos, Carter and Doc stood towering over Glorious and Josie in fancy long gowns, while Pastor Hankerson led them through the binding oaths. Carter never saw either the bride or groom so happy as they grinned out over the small audience of family and a few church members witnessing the beginning of their life together.

Years before, Doc had made it clear that he wanted to come out of the Army with a good-paying trade. . In Korea, he had helped build roads and air strips. He often said, "I f-f-f-fought for the American flag, so I should get sumpn that lasts outa that." What he got was the training and experience required to operate all kinds of heavy construction machinery. He drove tractors, graders, backhoes, and earth movers, all sorts of big machines

Doc became one of the few black heavy equipment operators on the Monterey Peninsula, and he built a solid reputation that put him in high demand. He bought a used tractor-trailer truck for hauling his

107

backhoe and D-8 Caterpillar tractor, and he worked everywhere--in Seaside, Monterey, Pacific Grove, and Carmel, even in places like Salinas, Gilroy and San Jose. He worked hard, doing extra jobs on some weekends and holidays. And he made really good money. His industriousness and Glorious's thriftiness enabled them to build and pay for their big, comfortable house--four bedrooms, a sunken living room, a formal dining room and an attached three-car garage.

And Doc raved about "his babies" as Glorious birthed each of their children. "Ain't-ain't-ain't he cute?" Or,

"She's more like her m-m-mama than any of em."

He loved that they all looked like both parents--darker than their mother but lighter than their father, their shapes and features more or less like one or the other of their parent's. More than once, Carter's mother Sarah laughed and said about Doc's child worship,

"I guess every crow thinks his crow's the whitest."

"I g-g-got babies now. I can't be shuckin and jivin no more now. It's up to me to make bread and provide em a place," Doc would say.

When Baby Doc and Jenelle were taken, Doc tried to die too. He wept for months, lost weight he couldn't afford to lose off his skinny frame, and was deeply depressed for even longer.

"Wh-why did I have to lose my babies? They-they didn't do nothin to nobody. It jus ain't right for parents to have to bury their kids."

Glorious's fear that he might hurt himself in his despair nearly overrode her own grief.

Sitting at the kitchen table in the house that Doc built while his widow talked on the phone, Carter flashed back to that horrible, horrible day, the worst in his life after that day his father, Reverend Hankerson, died suddenly. Just over five years before this day, Carter and Claudia had brought their children down to Seaside to visit their grandmother

108

Sarah. She so doted on those kids after the Reverend died that she reminded Carter a little of Mother Sally Wilson.

The telephone had rung then in the Hankerson house, just as it had this afternoon this afternoon in the house that Doc built. Carter discovered the caller was Glorious. Without a greeting or any other kind of introduction, she blurted out,

"Satch, you gotta go find Doc. He's doin some job down in Carmel Valley and he should have been back long before now. He said he'd be home before three o'clock, and it's almost six now. You gotta go find him." There was no panic in her voice or manner--just straight, hard information, boom, boom, boom.

When he got to the Jackson house, Glorious gave him directions to the new housing development going up in the Valley. He drove too fast over Carmel Hill and headed east down the Valley. The directions Glorious gave him took him right to the project. Way back against a corner of one of the few paved streets already in, Carter saw Doc's truck but only a bit of the Caterpillar. Part of one track jutting up at a strange angle.

He skidded his car to a stop in front of the truck without seeing Doc or anyone else moving around the big rig. Carter's stomach sank. He jumped out and ran around to the curb side of the truck where what he saw nearly knocked him to his knees. There Doc was, crushed beneath one of the tracks on his tractor. His eyes bulged out and his mouth was twisted grotesquely. A trickle of blood ran out onto the ground and formed a dark, dried puddle around his face. Most of his body was still under the huge machine.

Carter understood immediately what must have happened: while Doc was driving the Cat up the ramps up onto the truck bed, the left-hand ramp had broken, wrenching the big machine around so fast and hard that it fell off the truck and rolled over. Doc had tried to leap clear of the tumbling tractor, but failed to jump far enough. And while the damp soil cushioned the falling man and machine, there was not nearly enough sponginess to absorb the extreme force coming down. The tons of steel caught Doc and crushed the life out of him.

Carter fell to his knees trembling and heaving up his lunch. He cradled the lifeless head of his friend in his arms. He wept and swore at the injustice and unfairness of it all. How terrible that moment must have been! What must he have thought? Why Doc, a good man who was always busy and careful? Carter never tracked how long he knelt there with his dead friend. Recognizing darkness and the fog bank approaching, he finally pulled himself up and stumbled to his car to go for help.

Time telescoped into a blur of activity that felt like it would never end. Police cars and aid vans whirling around the wreck. Carter crying and trying to explain again and again what he discovered, when and how. Carter and Claudia trying to comfort Glorious and the children, their own shock and grief breaking them down periodically. Church members stopping in at the Jackson house and a few staying overnight just to be there to help. Memorial planning that thrust Carter back into the memories of burying his father. The weeping Glorious's jumping out of her seat at Doc's funeral to run silently around the church auditorium wringing her hands until some of the ushers gathered her up, fanning and comforting her in a corner.

Coming back into the kitchen, Glorious said,

"That was the foreman--actually a woman--from the laundry out at Fort Ord calling to see if Lena could get there to fill out papers and everything in the next couple days. Looks she could start to work there fulltime next Monday. I hope she'll do it, cause Lord knows I need her to get a steady job so she can take care of herself and her daughter."

"Is Cheri still working for the schools," Carter asked.

110

"Yeah. But now she's at the office in downtown Monterey. She coordinates part of the teacher's aide program. She puts teachers and aides together so they can figure out who's going where--you know, which teachers and aides work together at the different schools. Cheri's not like Lena about work. She can keep a job all right. She just can't keep her clothes on and her legs together." Glorious and Carter shared a short, ironic laugh and a shake of the head.

She went on,

"That girl's a mess. I mean, she's got these three kids here and still never been married. And a couple of months ago she was running around here all scared and talking about abortion cause she was afraid she was pregnant again." She paused briefly. "I'm telling you, as much as I miss him, I'm glad their daddy's not here to see how these girls he was so crazy about have turned out."

"Yeah, I still miss him a lot too," Carter mused.

"I don't know what I woulda done if I was the first one to find him all mashed under that big old tractor like you did," she said glancing up at Carter.

Once started, she seemed unable to stop, as if she were telling the story for the first time to someone who didn't know it.

"I tried my best to get him not to go out there to Carmel Valley to do that job by himself that day. But, no, he just had to go and do it. You know how stubborn he was. I can still hear him, 'N-n-n-naw, Baby. Th-th-this ain't no big deal. All I got to do is d-d-d-dig them big old tree stumps out, then grade the bed for the driveway. B-b-be home before three o'clock.' And look what happened. I don't know how old that ramp was, but I know he bought all that stuff used and had it a long time." Her voice trailed off to nearly a whisper.

"I guess sometimes you just don't know."

111

Tears streamed down her cheeks and met under her chin. Silently, Carter took her left hand in both of his, stroking it slowly, moving her wedding band gently with each stroke.

"Crazy boy," she muttered through her tears. "Stubborn too."

Fighting back his own tears, Carter said brightly, hoping to change the mood,

"God, Glorious, remember that time you and Doc came up to meet Claudia and me at my folks' place on Lake Berryessa? We'd just come back from our wedding trip to Reno and stopped to spend a week on the lake. Josie and James kept Little Doc and Cheri. That's the time you caught that huge catfish, almost twenty pounds. We just skinned that rascal out and sliced thick boneless steaks off of him."

"Oh, yeah. And Doc kept on sayin he could water ski on his bare feet. Crazy thing."

"And he almost did, too," put in Carter. "I'll never forget how surprised he looked when the boat pulled him into the water head first.

They both laughed loudly for a few minutes. Glorious dried her eyes and blew her nose. Then she said,

"We got to be quiet, Satch. I don't want them babies wakin up yet." Then she went on a bit quieter, "And that day you came skiin up to the shore."

"Oh, shit, Glo. Don't bring that up," said Carter.

She kept on, "You'd been skiin all around, playin and showin out, just havin a good old time. You had been telling Doc to drop you off out from the shore, and then you'd swim in.

"Only that last time, while Doc swooped the boat in a circle towards the shore, you decided to hang onto the rope until the last minute and ride right up to the shore and step out of the ski onto the ground. Like some of those people on TV do."

112

Through his laughter, Carter took up the story, "I was doing just fine except I came in too fast. So when the ski hit the mud, it stuck and shot me up the bank like I was coming out of a gun. I let myself ride it out and skidded to a stop on my belly." More laughter.

Glorious said,

"And when you stood up, you were skinned from your chin down to your toes. I mean you were one big scrape. Poor Claudia, just married and everything, started crying cause she was scared you might have been hurt bad."

"And crazy old Doc tied up the boat and came over and looked at me. Then he said, 'D-d-d-damn! Motherfucker, y-y-you ain't supposed to try to water ski on dry land. Even I know that.'" More laughter until Carter ended the recollection,

"My buddy, my buddy." They both puffed a little, remembering in their own ways.

Glorious took them back to where they had left their subject.

"If Doc saw how his 'babies' carry on, I don't know what he'd say or do. One of em has three babies and no husband anywhere to be seen. I'm not sure she even knows exactly who their daddies are. And she jus drops em on me to take care of without even askin. I mean she comes in from work, takes her shower and she's gone. 'Don't wait up, Mom,' she hollers and she's out the door. And I don't see her again until morning when she's getting ready to go to work.

"Sometimes on weekends, she drags home whatever old guy she's running around with. I know they stay here over night sometimes when I'm at work. If I'm here, I just make sure all the kids are taken care of and go to my room and watch TV or read my Bible. Then that younger one Lena, sometimes she stumbles in here so drunk, high or whatever that she can barely make it to her room. I can hear her in the bathroom throwing up. She's a wreck. Sometimes I just don't know what to do."

"Glo, you don't have to put up with that kind of crap. You're sixty years old and this is your house. What you say ought to be law here."

She came back, "That's what Clara Meeks says. You know how she can be. The other day, she stood right over there in front of the refrigerator with her hands on her hips and said, 'Glorious, you shouldn't take no mess like that from them gals. You should put they stinky behins out.' But Doc always said that as long as he had a home, his 'babies' had a home. I don't know what he'd do if he was here today."

They both went silent for what seemed like a long time. Leaning over so he could see out the window into the fog then glancing at his watch, Carter said,

"So, Glorious, you still haven't told me what happened to your clocks. I remember when Doc got you the first one. I've always liked the way you've talked about collecting them--'saving time.' That's nice. So what happened?"

Slowly, quietly, Glorious began telling Carter the story. She came home after a three-day sick bed vigil at her employer, Mrs. Holland's, house. It appeared that the invalid was dying, but she survived the crisis. The exhausted Glorious returned to a wrecked house. Cheri shame facedly told her mother what happened. She and her boyfriend came into the house drunk and angry. They started fighting and in the struggle knocked down the clock rack, damaging or destroying all five clocks. Making matters worse, Cheri grabbed up Glorious's favorite one and threw it at him, missing him and breaking the clock beyond repair. Glorious ended the story,

"I guess it just goes to show careless people are dangerous."

Next, Glorious seemed to perk up a little, to speak with a bit more resolve. She said,

"I know what I'm going to do."

114

"What's that?" asked Carter.

"I'm not going to tell you right now. You'll find out soon enough. You want some more coffee?"

"No, thanks. It's getting to time for me to move. We're leaving for home in the morning, and I should spend the rest of this day with Mom."

"Oh, yeah. I know she wants to spend every minute she can with you guys and her grandbabies even if they aren't babies any more. And I need to be gettin organized to fix dinner for my crew. It's about time for that bossy little Doris to come stompin in here draggin that nasty blanket, 'Nana, Doh eat, Doh eat, Nana.' That little sister might not be able to talk too good yet, but she can sure make you know what she wants."

She got up from the table and took a pink envelope from a partly full basket on the counter beneath a cupboard. She laid it down in front on Carter. He noticed his name and address written on the front in her tiny, meticulous hand. It had a stamp on it.

"This is a letter I wrote to Cheri and Lena, and I wanted you to have a copy of it." Glorious said, "I didn't know you were comin by today. That's why it's all addressed and stamped and everything."

A bit confused, Carter said,

"A letter? Why a letter and why me?"

"Well," she answered, "a letter just felt right to me. I've talked to these girls until my voice is hoarse and my face is blue. But they don't change, so I wrote them. I mailed each one a copy of it yesterday, so they should get them by Friday. But you can't read yours until after you leave."

Carter hesitated briefly. He wondered what was in it, but since Glorious had said it was written to her daughters, he figured she was just giving it to him for information. He shoved it into his jacket pocket as he stood up to go.

115

"Okay," was all he said. He put on his San Francisco Giants baseball cap and moved to leave. At the front door, he wrapped her up again in a tight squeeze and held her for a moment. Then after giving her a peck on the neck, he said,

"See ya, Glorious," and went down the steps to the sidewalk and his car.

"Bye, Satch," she answered.

Carter drove up Maple Street and across Noche Buena Avenue, the scented pink envelope on the seat beside him. He pulled over into the first easy parking space he saw. He turned off his car's engine and opened the letter. More of the same tight, tiny handwriting as on the envelope said,

Dear Cheri and Lena,

You may be surprised to be getting a letter from me since we're a mother and her daughters all living in the same house. But writing this down has helped make everything clearer to me, and I hope it will do the same for you. Also, you can read this over as many times as you want to so you can be sure to understand everything. I'm moving into my own place. That means you're going to have to get your child care from someone else. I still love both of you and your precious babies, but I just can't live in the house with you. I'm too old and tired, and I've suffered too much. I'm over sixty years old and I need more control of the rest of my life if I can get it. We've talked about our problems together over and over again, but all talking seems to do is make everyone mad. And I'm not mad now. Just tired.

I don't mean to insult you, but you need to know what I'm talking about. You don't pay rent or help with the utilities or food. You expect

116

me to baby sit all the time. You don't even ask if it's all right or nothing. And you don't offer to pay me or do anything special to show me your thanks. You know that your ways of being with men, alcohol and drugs are against what I believe. I'm saved and I don't approve of any of that. I thought of putting you out. But you know what your daddy always said--if he had a home, his babies had a home. He's gone now, but I'm making sure his promise still stands. He saw to it that the house is paid for, so all you'll ever have to pay for is taxes and upkeep. You're both grown, so you can do what you want. I just don't have to be involved in it.

I've rented and furnished myself an apartment out in Marina, and when I get off from work at Mrs. Holland's after this weekend, that's where I'll go. My phone number is 831-789-1357. After we've all had a chance to get used to our new situations, I'll have you over to visit me in my new place. Meantime, feel free to call me when you want to, and I'll stop by from time to time.

I'm giving Satch and Claudia Hankerson my contacts. He was Doc's closest friend, and the two of them are my closest ones, so we'll be in touch with each other. Their number in San Francisco is 415-943-4849, so you can call them if you need to.

I hope you girls take hold of yourselves and build the kinds of lives you want for yourselves and your children. I also hope you'll understand that I'm not making this move to hurt or punish you or anything like that. I'm doing it so I can breathe deep again. I love you and your babies very much. You are, after all, my family. I'll pray for you, and if you pray sometimes, please pray for me.

117

Your Mother Glorious (Gloria)

"Oh, shit!" Carter thought to himself. All the strength and energy seemed to leave his body, and a light sweat popped out on his forehead.

Oh, shit!" he mumbled again, his mouth dry. Pictures and snippets of conversations with Doc and Glorious moved across his mind as if they were on a movie screen, making him feel much like he had when he found Doc's dead body. How had that stolid, shy, little block of a woman come to this place? Simple, deep, truthful words--how like her. Poor Glorious. Poor daughters. Poor grandbabies. What would Doc have thought or done about this? What would those girls do?

He sat still and silent for a few more minutes, staring out into the foggy gloom. Finally, he let out a big sigh and started his engine. He said out loud into the chilly air, "Why not?" and drove away towards his mother's house.

Anything for Me?

"Anything for me today?"

"No, Mom. Just relax there in bed."

"I mean am I supposed to do anything today?"

"I know. No. Just relax and try to get better, build up your strength. Right now your blood pressure's too high, your sugar's all out of whack and your heart's not beating right. That's why you're trembling so much—it's a kind of palsy."

"Ain't no church tonight?"

"No."

"Am I supposed to do anything tonight?"

"Just the same thing you're doing now—just resting in bed. You have what they call hypercalcemia, which means excessive calcium in your system. That's causing you all those problems I just talked about. It makes your heart speed up, slow down and even skip beats—arhythmia they call that. It makes you weak so you can't walk very well. Remember you've fallen down several times here lately? And you're not as young as you used to be, so you can't be falling down and carrying on. It's the high calcium that keeps you confused and disoriented so you don't recognize people you should know and can't figure out where you are."

"How old am I again?"

"You're almost ninety."

"My Lord! No wonder I'm havin' so much trouble. What's today's name?"

"Tuesday."

119

"Tuesday. I know you told me, but I done forgot. I don't go to church tonight, do I?"

"No. If you're better, maybe you can go to church Sunday."

"So I'm not supposed to do anything tonight?"

"Yes. You're supposed to eat, sleep and take your medicine. We need to build you up for your surgery tomorrow. That'll fix a couple of your glands and your hypercalcemia. Then you can go home in a few days.

"Hey, Mom. Don't pull that out of your arm. That's your IV giving you medicine to help you get better. You have to leave that alone."

"How come they have all that tape and stuff on my arm?"

"That's how they keep the IV needle in place. They use it to put medicine and nutrients into your body without your having to take a lot of shots and pills and things."

"What if I don't want medicine and nutrients?"

"Well, I guess you just have to have them right now whether you want them or not. That's all to help you get better."

"Hey, Mister. Who left the door open and let in all those white people out there in my kitchen? Who are they? Who let them in?"

"Those are the nurses and doctors and other people who work here. And that isn't your kitchen out there."

"What is it, then?"

"The nurse's station."

"Where am I?"

"The hospital."

"The hospital?"

"Yes."

"No I'm not. This is my house, and my husband's right upstairs there sleepin."

"No, Mom. This is the hospital. And I'm sorry, but your husband has been dead for over twenty years."

"Hospital? This ain't no hospital. This is my house on Maple Street, and my husband is right upstairs sleepin."

"I wish both of those things were true. But I'm afraid they're not. You just don't remember. That's all."

"Where are all of my people? The colored people? Ain't none of my people comin' to see about me?"

"Sure. I'm one of your people. I'm your child, and that's why I'm here. To see about you. Your other son will be here tonight."

"Ha, ha, ha! I don't know who you are, Mister, but you sure ain't none of my children. Don't you think I know my own children?"

"Don't you recognize me? I flew all the way here to see and be with you. I'm your oldest child."

"You look kind of like my children and sound like em, but you ain't none of them. I'm forgetful, but I ain't crazy. I know my own children, honey. After all I went through to bring those kinkyheads into this world and then raise em up, you know good and well I know who my children are."

"You don't recognize me, but I'm your son."

"How come more of my people ain't here? Some other ones beside you, I mean."

"Oh, I don't know for sure. I guess some of them are working, and some of them are out of town. Some are doing other things, so I'm with you right now. But some others will come see you before too long."

"Look like all my family and frens done gone and lef me here by myself. Mama and Dad, my sister Willie Mae, Mother Wilson, Sista and Brotha Brown. I don't know who all."

"Yeah, you've outlived a lot of folks."

121

"How old did you say I am?"

"Nearly ninety."

"My Lord, almost ninety. No wonder so many folks have gone on ahead of me. How long have I been like this. I mean how long have I had this All-hammers?"

"I think it must be somewhere around twenty years."

"Think I'm ever goin back to bein like I was before this?"

"I think you're going to get better after your operation, but I don't think you're going back to being like you were when you were fifty. I'm afraid all of us in this life are on a one-way street and can't go back."

"Ain't that something?"

"Hey, don't pull that tape off. Don't pull that needle out of your arm. Remember, Mom? That's your IV, and you have to keep that in your arm so you can keep getting medicine and stuff to help you get better."

"Who said I have to keep all this mess in my arm?"

"Your doctor."

"I don't see no doctor here. I'm gonna take this thing off. I don't need no mess like this."

"No, Mom. You have to leave that in."

"No, I don't either."

"Yes, you do."

"Who says so?"

"Your doctor. And I do too.."

"I don't care 'bout no doctor. And you neither. You ain't none of my papa. I'm gonna take this off."

"No, Mom. Do you want me to come hold your hands? I don't want to, but I will if you keep trying to take that IV out."

"You can't make me do nothin."

"Stop, Mom. Stop right now!"

122

"Turn me a loose. Quit holdin me."

"Not until you leave that IV alone. You're going to make a mess, and we don't need that now."

"Lord Jesus. Can't even take this old mess off and go home. Unh, unh, unh. I don't know your name, but whoever you are, don't never get old and sick like me. I'm tellin you, it's pitiful."

"I'm sorry you feel that way, but I'm just trying to do what I can to help you get well enough to go home. There. That's better. Just relax and rest. You'll feel a lot better if you do."

"So I don't have anything to do tonight?"

"Just eat, sleep and try to get better."

"And I don't go nowhere tonight-- church or nowhere?"

"No. You just stay here and build up for your surgery tomorrow. After that, you can go home in a few days."

"I'm not at home right now? And my husband's not sleepin upstairs?"

"Right. I'm sorry, but you're not at home and your husband is in heaven. You're in the hospital"

"The hospital, hunh?"

"Yes."

"When can I go home?"

"I don't know exactly. You have to get better first. Then you can go home—probably in a few days."

"What's today's name?"

"This is Tuesday."

"Did you tell me where this is, what this place is?"

"Yes. This is the hospital. The Community Hospital."

"Who are all those white people in there? Did they come in the back door when wasn't nobody lookin?"

"No, they work here. They're doctors and nurses and people like that."

"What do they do?"

"They take care of you so you can get better faster and then go home. Here's a nurse now. She has some medicine for you."

"It's Tylenol for your pain, Sweetie. Do you have any pain? Just swallow these down with this water. Slow, slow, now. There you go. Good for you, Dear. Here, let me straighten you around in bed a little bit. There you go. Isn't that better?"

"Do I go anywhere today?"

"No. You just stay here and let us take care of you so you can get better and go home."

"When can I go home, to my own house?"

"I don't know for sure, but your doctor will tell us when you can go. I'll come back in and check on your later. OK?"

"I guess so, but I'm ready to go home."

"I know, Mom."

"Here's the physical therapist. His name is Bob. He wants you to sit up on the side of your bed and then stand up for a little bit. You need to build up your strength so you can get through your surgery tomorrow and heal up fast. Then you can use your walker to get around when we get you home."

"Good morning there. Are we going to sit on the side of the beddy-bed and then stand up for me so I can see what a strong girl we are?"

"What if I don't want to sit up on the side of the bed or stand up?"

"Well, you don't have to, darlin, but that wouldn't be good for you. You have to be able to sit up and stand up in order to be able to go home."

"Is this what I'm supposed to do?"

"Yes. Thatta girl. That's exactly what you're supposed to do. You're so strong. Look at you. That was great. Oh, you're making my day, Precious. We're going to have you up and out of here in no time. I'll come back again later. You just sit up and stand up whenever you feel like it, Dearie. 'Bye now."

"How much longer do I have to do this? I mean sit here on the side of the bed like this."

"Not much longer. When I talked to him earlier, Bob said you just had to do it for about fifteen minutes or so. Just stay up for a little bit longer, and then you can lie back down. Hey, don't pull that IV out of your arm. Do we have to start wrestling again? Remember?"

"Lord, lord. Am I ever goin home? I don't think I'm ever goin home again."

"Sure, you are. You just have to get better and stronger and then you can go home to your own house, your own bed and all of your own things."

"Well, I guess I'll just lie here then."

"That's all right. Just relax and rest. That's the best thing for you. And I'll stay right here in case you need anything."

"Is there anything for me to do today?"

"No, Mom."

"Tonight?"

"No."

"I'm not supposed to go to church or nothin?"

"No, this is Tuesday. Sunday is the day you go to church."

"So I'm not supposed to do nothin?"

"No."

"Nothin?"

"Nothing."

About the Author

S. R. "Rudy" Martin, Jr. was a founding faculty member of The Evergreen State College in Olympia, Washington. He taught American/African American Studies and was an administrator there until he retired in 1997. His previous major publications are the family memoir *On the Move: A Black Family's Western Saga (2009)* and the novel *Natural Born Proud: A Revery* (2010.

126

These are truly stories from the heart about "the human heart in conflict with itself." Creating a set of vivid and memorable characters, centered around Carter Hankerson and the Hankerson family in northern California, S.R. Martin, Jr. presents a compact cycle of indelible vignettes about growing up black in middle-class America in the mid-twentieth century. These stories explore themes of love, loyalty, friendship, compassion, ambition, pride, self-doubt, rebellion, race, responsibility, and forgiveness. Narrated in unique and distinctive voices, masculine, feminine, and graphic, they maintain an easy harmony between narration and dialogue. Race, music, and religion loom large in all these stories. "Sunday Songs," "Glorious," and "Anything for Me?" guide us down a path the author knows well and has illuminated with skill and compassion. There is much to be learned by spending a while in Seaside through these stories.

Thomas Grissom, author of *The Physicist's World*, and *Parodies of the Fall*.

128